A
Place
for
Troy

Ernie + Betty
Thank you for your
friendship. No two people
have ever made such a
long lasting impression on
us.
"Dare to Dream"
Love
Judy
+ Daisy

May 15, 2000

A Place for Troy

by

Judy A. Crawford

ISBN: 1-55517-490-6
v.1

Published by Bonneville Books

Distributed by:
925 North Main, Springville, UT 84663 • 801/489-4084

CFI Publishing and Distribution Since 1986

Cedar Fort, Incorporated
CFI Distribution • CFI Books • Council Press • Bonneville Books

Typeset by Virginia Reeder
Cover design by Adam Ford
Cover design © 2000 by Lyle Mortimer

Printed in the United States of America

Chapter One

Troy Berringer stood in the center of his little bedroom. His arms ached and his body and mind were weary. He had no energy left to finish unpacking the boxes he and his brothers had deposited on the bed.

Troy looked around. Even in the subdued lighting the cracks in the cream-colored ceiling and the stains on the thin green carpet were visible. I don't believe this, he thought. I can't believe we're here. Living in a place like this? We should be on the farm. The grain would be thick and green, the canola a rich yellow, and the strawberry and raspberry plants red with fruit. Mom would be hoeing the garden and Dad and I cutting hay and fighting over the piano. This, he swept the room with his eyes, is not the place for me.

He shuffled over to a packing box and ripped open the lid. The blue baseball cap lay right on top. Troy snatched it up and looked at it for a moment before crumpling it tightly and flinging it into the back of the closet. He stared after it as if it were going to leap back out at him. A crash on the floor above him made him jump.

"Stop it, Alan!" Troy heard his brother, David, yell. Taking the steps two at a time, Troy was up the stairs in a moment.

Another crash... "Alan!" David lunged at his brother, pinning him onto the bed just as Troy entered the bedroom.

"Hey! What's going on?"

"Alan's at it again!" David struggled to hold the wildly contorting body.

Troy grabbed his little brother's shoulder. "Alan! Stop it!" A leg caught Troy in the chest. "Alan! Stop!" This time Alan stopped. Slowly David released the boy. "Now, what's up?" Troy asked, pulling Alan to his feet.

"Nothin'." Alan jerked away.

"Oh no?" David bent to pick up pieces of plastic from the floor. "Then why'd you chuck the models?"

"I don't want them anymore." Alan's blue eyes glared, his tight light brown curls dark with moisture.

"But..." David started, holding the bits and pieces in front of him.

Alan smacked them out of his hand. "I don't want 'em! I hate 'em!"

"Okay, that's enough." Troy shook his youngest brother while motioning David away with a flip of his head. "You're supposed to be unpacking, Alan. Quietly, so you won't wake up Mom." He let go of Alan, who slumped away.

"I don't want those dumb models," he continued to protest.

David was picking up the broken pieces again. "But Dad helped you build them," he said.

Alan lunged at David again. Troy grabbed him from behind. "If you wake up Mom, I'll clobber you! Do you hear?" Alan fell back onto the bed.

"Is there a problem?" Joanie Berringer stood in the doorway, her head resting against the frame. Her face was pale, her hollow eyes heavy beneath dishevelled hair.

Troy scowled at Alan. "Nothing we can't handle, Mom," he said matter-of-factly as he stood before her, his 5 foot 11 inch frame tall and straight.

Alan was on the floor cleaning up now. David discarded the handful of plastic into the small trash can in the corner.

"Sorry we woke you," David said. "We've almost finished unpacking." His thick dark eyebrows lifted, wrinkling his broad forehead. His brown eyes darted around the room. "It's lookin' okay, isn't it?"

Joanie stepped inside. Troy and David moved to let her through. They looked at each other then at their mother. Joanie lifted Alan to his feet. His white face relaxed, his tight lips quivered.

"You'll have to learn to control that temper, son." Her words were kind. "It'll only make things worse."

Alan looked up at his mother then wrapped his arms around her waist and sobbed into the cotton pullover she wore. Joanie pressed him to her but spoke to the other boys.

"I'm going to make some supper. David, will you help me? Troy, Alan could use some help unpacking the last of his boxes."

Both David and Troy nodded, but neither moved until Joanie had released Alan.

Troy and Alan worked in silence as they folded T-shirts and shorts and placed them in the dresser drawer. Troy opened the last box. Right on top sat four model cars with colorfully painted decals advertising motor oils of every brand. He lifted one out.

"I don—" Alan went to grab it away. Troy pulled back.

"Don't break anymore, Alan." Troy took the car and set it on the bed. "You worked hard to build these." Troy ruffled Alan's hair, often envying the natural curl that he had inherited from his father. "Let's put them on the shelf in your closet so you can see them if you want to, but where they won't always be looking at you."

Alan picked up the car Troy had set aside, turned it in his hands, and handed it to Troy. Soon the boxes were empty. Troy stacked them together and turned to leave. Alan stood quiet, eyeing the bits and pieces of plastic in the trash can. Troy had moved toward the door; now he came back to Alan.

"Come on," he said, "let's go eat. I can help you build some more."

Alan's forlorn look made a lump fill Troy's throat. "Can we find some just like these?" Alan asked.

Troy nodded his response. Together the two boys made their way to the supper table. The two boys were so much like each other, and so much like their father. Alan even had his father's curly sandy hair; Troy had the same coloring but not the curl.

Troy watched his mother while they ate. She moved the food around on her plate, eating only the odd tidbit. Her eyes were bright beneath her nearly black curls, and she smiled as she talked, but Troy was very aware of the stress she was under and the pain she suffered. They had talked several times since the funeral, and even though she seemed positive most days, she couldn't hide her loss and fears. Troy's father had always taken care of her, especially after she got the diabetes. Troy knew he could not do what his father did. He did want to help though, and tried to remember how his father had handled various situations. However, like tonight with Alan, Troy felt very inadequate.

Troy looked longingly at the piano. Maybe it wasn't the best solution, but he had always found comfort in music. The love for music he had inherited from his father. Ray Berringer, with all his male roughness, had loved the piano. Troy got up from the table and stood by the bench his father had built. As a child he remembered sitting at the end of a long day on his father's knee on the large bench, watching and listening. Grease embedded the deep crevices in his father's thick fingers, which were almost too big for a piano player. Dirt lingered under his short, chipped fingernails even after an intense scrubbing.

Troy loved to hear the songs his father played from the

church hymn book, but it was the songs from the 60's that Troy loved most. Even the modern songs he tried now didn't have the appeal that the songs of his father's era had: Simon and Garfunkel's "Bridge Over Troubled Water," The Platters' "Great Pretender," music from the classics and movies, even some country and western. When teasing his wife, Ray would pounce noisily through a Beatles medley, knowing all the while how she disliked their popularity.

This was how Troy began playing—plunking a few notes once he had heard his father play. Ray realized Troy's talent and would play slowly so Troy could hear the melody then copy it. Troy's ability to listen then play was incredible. It was only the last few years that his father was actually teaching him to read music.

The house was quiet when Troy slid onto the piano bench later that night. David and Alan were in their room and Joanie was in the bathroom preparing for bed. Relieved to be at the piano, Troy began to play. At first he fingered the song facing him from the open book, but he quickly reverted to the familiar melodies he knew by heart—melodies he had learned from his father. He closed his eyes, the words of "Song For The Asking" softly escaping his lips. "Here is my song for the asking. Ask me and I will play. This is my tune for the taking. Take it, don't turn away." Paul Simon must have known Ray Berringer when he wrote and sang that song. The words were so much like him: a giving person, and very loving. The words rolled round in Troy's head. "Ask me and I will play. All the love I hold inside." Troy sat quietly for a moment, his cheeks warm, his fingers shaky. What could he do with all the love he held inside, all the love he had for his father and his father for him? How could he live without his dad? He didn't wipe away the tears on his cheeks. Other images filled Troy's mind. He tried to shake them away...

Troy could see the small chapel filled to capacity and the flower-laden mahogany coffin positioned in front of the podium. His fingers began to play as he remembered. Troy could see his father lying as though asleep under the white satin. His hands, weather-worn and rough, were folded across his waist. In his mind Troy reached out to touch his father's hand. Those fingers would never again touch the ivory keys and make them sing. Troy was crying now, his head resting on the keyboard, the music silent.

"Troy?" Joanie placed her hand on Troy's shoulder. "Come on, son. It's late."

Troy wiped away the tears before turning around. Joanie gave her son a gentle squeeze and a knowing smile but said nothing more. Troy pulled the cover over the keys, shutting off more than the music.

Back in his room Troy stood for a long time trying to understand all that had taken place, all that he felt. He glanced around the room then went to the closet. He lifted the tattered navy cap from off the floor. Sitting down on the bed again he turned the cap in his hands, his thumbs smoothing the crooked brim. Just holding it made his father seem closer. He revelled in the feeling for a few seconds and then he was back on the farm, sprinting down the red shale driveway, the water cooler swinging with every stride. He could hear the grind and groan of the tractor and the rattle of the mower as his father cut the grass in the wide, shallow ditch just beyond the Lombardy poplars and evergreens that lined the Berringer property.

Troy slowed to a trot, the water jug growing heavy in the hot sun. He wiped beads of sweat from his face with the sleeve of his shirt as he cut through the trees to reach his father quicker.

Ray Berringer stood on the tractor, one hand on the steering wheel, the other on the gear release for the mower. Troy waved but his father did not see him. The tractor was high on the incline, the blade on the mower he was pulling raised occasionally to cut into nothing.

Suddenly the tractor lurched, the right wheels lifting off the ground. Ray grabbed the steering wheel with both hands to keep his footing. His navy blue cap fell from his head as the motion of the mower propelled forward. The tractor tilted more. Troy began to run. "Dad!" he cried, dropping the water cooler. The tractor jerked violently again. Ray was thrown to the ground. The tractor leaned sharply and turned. The motor screamed, the mower blade rattled, slicing the air. "No!" Troy shouted. Snatching up the cap that had fallen clear, Troy ran toward the overturned tractor. It howled wildly. "Dad!" Troy shouted again.

At first he couldn't see his father, then he spotted the red polka dot handkerchief jutting out of the pocket of the bib-overalls. Troy reached in and turned off the key. The motor ground to a halt.

"Dad?" Troy fell to his knees. Ray Berringer was only partially visible under the large tractor tire. "Dad?" Troy whispered, touching the dirt-streaked cheek. That was how Joanie Berringer found him, the navy blue cap still clutched in his hand.

Chapter Two

With the help of the bishop of the Inglewood ward, Troy had gotten a job at the local hardware store. Robert Matthews, one of the members of the ward, managed the business and felt Troy's knowledge of farming would be an asset.

Troy had been working at the hardware for over a week when his mother asked him about his duties. "I saw Robert Matthews at church today", Joanie said as she and Troy were cleaning up after lunch. "He says you fit right in at the hardware store."

Troy turned to face her. "I really enjoy it. Mr. Matthews is a nice guy to work for." Troy rinsed the last suds from the sink. "He even said I can work full time till school starts, then he'll use me on the weekends and on shipping days."

Joanie hung up her tea towel. "What does he have you doing?"

Troy wadded up the dishrag and threw it in the sink. "I sweep lots and restock shelves, mostly. Several times Mr. Matthews lets me fill lumber orders for the customers. He says I'll probably end up in the yard though, cutting and moving lumber."

"Is that a problem?" Joanie could tell her son was

thinking deeply.

Troy wiped his hands on his pants before speaking. "I hope not. I've run the tractors on the farm, but..." he couldn't finish the sentence.

"But what...is something wrong?"

Troy's head dropped. "I guess it's too much like a tractor." He swallowed hard. "I don't know if..."

Joanie gave his arm a reassuring squeeze. "When the time comes, Troy. I know you'll do fine."

"I—I hope so." Troy started for the dining room without looking up. "Anyway, Mr. Matthews hasn't asked me to drive yet." He walked away.

"Troy?" Troy stopped. "I didn't see you at the sacrament table this morning. Was there a reason you didn't help the priesthood?"

Troy spun around. "I didn't think I needed to do that. It's not our ward."

Joanie approached him. "It is our ward, now. This is our home."

"It doesn't feel like it." He turned away then looked back. "Anyway, I thought a ward this size would have more boys my age."

"Yeah, that surprised me, too," David interjected, coming from the livingroom. "I can't believe there's so few guys.

"It doesn't matter how few or how many young men there are. You boys have a responsibility."

"I—I passed sacrament, Mom," David said—cautiously giving Troy a side glance.

"Humph! "Troy glared at his brother.

"Troy!"

"Sorry, Mom. I don't care if David did. I couldn't. I just find it hard to get up in front of strangers."

"They won't be strangers for long if we get involved." Joanie and David followed Troy as he moved toward the piano. "You are really needed here."

"I won't promise anything, but I'll work on it." Troy dropped to the piano bench. "I just have a hard time understanding why God could let some things happen and I guess I need time to work it out before I start doing things in His name." He turned, opened the piano and began to play.

It was a warm and sunny Tuesday when Troy entered the house after work. He had been at the hardware for two weeks now and enjoyed his job more and more each day—especially Mr. Matthews. He was told to call Robert Matthews "Mister" when they were at work, but other times he would be Brother Matthews. Troy found it difficult to call his boss Mister, but it was getting easier.

Troy hurried to his room and tossed his jacket onto his bed. Next to his pillow he saw a yellow plastic bag.

"I bought you some new Bermudas for the youth activity this evening," his mother told him from his doorway. "I knew your blue cut-offs were quite tattered."

Troy swiped up the yellow bag, whipped it off the bed and pitched it into the air as he would have a fork full of hay. "I told you on Sunday I didn't want to go." His voice was firm but not aggressive.

"All work and no play makes Troy a dull boy," Joanie chuckled, hoping Troy would be less tense.

"It's childish and probably boring."

"I wish you'd go. You need to try to have fun. Besides," Joanie added, "David wants to go."

"David can go. He doesn't need me." Troy stepped away from his mother. When he turned back, she had already left the room. Troy dropped to the bed. He just wanted to stay home and play the piano. However, at 6:15 Troy entered the livingroom wearing his new shorts. "Let's go," he said to David, who was watching T.V. Joanie looked up from the sofa where she was sharing a book with Alan. She didn't speak.

She just watched David jump up and happily grab his swim gear.

"Have fun," she said, mostly to herself, as the boys ran out the door.

There were five or six kids at the church when Troy and David arrived. Bishop Schmidt was talking to two girls. Troy noticed the brunette giggling as she talked. Dressed in bright orange and yellow matching shorts and shirt, she bounced up and down, her hands gesturing rapidly as she spoke. Her friend, a girl in a red and purple Hawaiian outfit, hair pulled back into a ponytail, listened quietly. She had a bag of groceries in her arms. David darted away and for a moment Troy stood alone, feeling very conspicuous and self-conscious in his new clothes.

"Hello, Troy," Bishop Schmidt greeted and immediately came toward him. Troy's jaw clenched and he grimaced. "Kristin and Shenade, have you met Troy?" Kristin grinned widely, skipping over to Troy. Shenade followed slowly, the grocery bag hiding any expression on her face.

"Kristin Ferguson, Shenade Johnson, I'd like you to meet Troy Berringer. He and his family have just moved into the crescent east of the church."

Troy stood frozen, his fists tight at his sides. "Hi," he said stiffly, trying to keep his eyes averted from either girl.

"Hi," they both responded at once.

"I'll leave the three of you while I find the advisors, then we can head out to the lake."

"Are you coming with us?" Kristin asked, her attention going to the bishop.

"Yes. Until we get a Young Men's leader, I'll be helping out. Shenade, where is your mother?"

"She's in the kitchen cutting vegetables for the shish—kabobs. She said she'd be coming shortly." Shenade's comments were directed at the bishop, but her eyes watched Troy. "I—I think I'll go see if she needs help," she said shyly and turned away.

"Wait for me," Kristin called. Giving Troy a Cheshire smile, she hurried after Shenade.

Troy breathed a sigh of relief. He was thankful that he was no longer the focus of the girls' attention.

"We're ready!" a male voice called. "Let's have a prayer before we go."

Troy turned to see David with a group of boys and two leaders. He was talking eagerly to another boy Troy recognized from Sunday. Timothy Carter stayed close to David as the opening prayer was said, and everyone loaded into cars. Troy was ushered into a van filled with noisy boys where he appeared to be the oldest. David was with three boys apparently his own age. As usual, the younger ones outnumbered the rest. The six or seven girls crammed into two other cars.

The evening air was calm and the surface of Inglewood Lake lay like a mirror on flat ground. Sunbathers dotted the beach on this warm evening and campers lined the green grass. There were no mountains, but the rolling hills around the lake were green and spotted with groves of large overgrown poplars and thick patches of willow. The sandy beach surprised Troy. Its wide expanse glistened a snowy white from the silver water line up to the thick, green, manicured lawn and evergreens that circled the lake. The young people burst from the vehicles and sprinted down the sand into the water. Squeals of joy filled the air and Troy couldn't help but smile. He stopped long enough to watch a speed boat and waterskier go by. Along one wharf, fishermen, who were standing on a collage of large boulders, were casting in their lines.

"Are you going to join us?" a voice asked from behind. Troy turned to see who was speaking. "I'm Mrs. Johnson, the Young Women's president. We're glad to have you here."

"It's a nice lake." Troy tried to put his nervousness aside and be courteous.

"We come often because it's so close to town. Why don't you join the young people while we prepare the food?"

Troy nodded as he meandered over to the lake where David was filling balloons with water. Soon he, too, was involved in a water balloon toss and frisbee baseball. For a while Troy actually enjoyed himself, but every time he laughed or started to horse around, a twinge of guilt caused him to pause. If it wasn't feelings of guilt, it was images of his father's dying face and the sounds of the screaming tractor.

Troy walked to the water's edge to watch the setting sun slip behind the brilliant orange clouds on the western horizon. Its reflection sent a golden path onto the flat surface of the lake. He walked toward it, stopping just short of the water.

"Beautiful isn't it," a female voice stated more than questioned.

Troy turned to see Shenade sitting on a swing a short distance away, paper and pencil in her hand. He caught a glimpse of a black and white sketch of the lake and a sailboat. "It's a nice place."

"Have you been here before?" Shenade laid her pencil down on her paper.

"No, but the sunsets on the farm were gorgeous, too,"

"I believe it, but I think that sunsets belong near water. Look at the reflection!" She made a wide sweep of her hand.

"It is neat." Troy fidgeted with his hands, wishing his bermudas had pockets. Shenade gave herself a push with her feet and the swing moved away. On its forward motion, she jumped clear and with two steps was standing beside Troy. Instinctively he moved away, picked up a handful of small stones, and began skipping them on the water. The golden path rippled and shimmered and Troy watched it settle and become smooth again.

"Are there more children in your family?" Shenade asked, coming to stand beside him again. "I know David is your brother."

"There are three of us. Alan's home with Mom. He's only eleven."

"What made you move to Inglewood? Did your dad get a job here?"

Shenade didn't miss the shudder of Troy's shoulders and the paling of his face. She stepped backward, her paper dropping to the sand. Troy looked at it, then at Shenade, then spun on his heel and ran down the beach in the opposite direction.

"Troy!" David called.

Shenade turned to see Troy's brother approaching, a hot shish-kabob in his hand.

"Hey, where's he going?" David asked.

"I just asked him a simple question and he immediately took off." Shenade glanced away from David and spotted Troy disappearing between the trees.

"What did you ask him?"

"I asked if your dad had a job in town."

David stiffened. "T—th—that'll do it," he said. "Dad died in a farm accident in May." His voice broke and he turned away.

Shenade gasped and started after him. "I didn't know. I'm so sorry."

David kept walking back toward the group of kids. When they got closer, he spoke, "I guess you'll have to eat this. I made it for Troy, but I don't think he's hungry."

Shenade took the wire. "I really am sorry, David. I didn't mean to hurt either of you."

"It's okay." David walked away, heading for the parking lot and some time alone.

Shenade watched David for a minute, then went in search of the bishop. She found him surrounded by a handful of playful boys. Bishop Schmidt noticed Shenade march toward him, shish-kabob held high. He looked from her to

Kristin, who was now following her friend.

"Excuse me," he said to the boys.

"Why didn't someone tell us before we made fools of ourselves?" Shenade asked when the bishop reached her side.

"Tell us what?" Kristin eyed her friend carefully.

Bishop Schmidt put his arms around both girls and guided them toward the beach. At the water's edge he released them and spoke. "I presume you're talking about Troy and David." Shenade nodded.

Glancing about anxiously, Kristin glanced from the bishop to her best friend. "What? What?" she asked.

"Yes," said Bishop Schmidt, "I haven't had a chance to talk to any of you about it. I wasn't expecting the boys to be here. Their mother didn't think they were coming."The bishop spoke hurriedly. "Did Troy tell you, Shenade?"

"Tell you what?" Kristin insisted, bouncing in front of the bishop.

Shenade shook her head. "No, David did. He said his father had died, but didn't give me any details."

"Ooh," whispered Kristin, her body suddenly still.

"Do you know what happened?" Shenade asked.

"It was a farm accident...a tractor roll over, I think." The bishop looked around to see who else was listening. Seeing they were alone he added. "Troy was with his father at the time."

"Oooh," Kristin sighed again.

The bishop started back toward the group. "Let's not advertise what we know and make the boys more self-conscious. Just try to make them part of the youth program in our ward. They'll talk about it when they're ready."

"It's too bad there aren't any boys Troy's age," Kristin said. "That might help."

"How do you know how old Troy is?" Shenade perked up slightly.

"I asked David. Troy's seventeen. David will be fifteen

on the fifteenth of August, and they have an eleven-year-old brother, Alan."

"I don't know how you do it," Shenade chuckled. "You're ahead of everyone."

"Just my personality," Kristin beamed.

Bishop Schmidt smiled, glad Kristin's humour lightened the scene. "Just be friends, not curiosity seekers."

"We will," Shenade told him as they returned to the group. Shenade looked around for Troy and David but didn't see them again until they were ready to leave. Neither boy spoke on the return trip to town.

Troy slammed the door as he entered the house.

"Hey!" David exclaimed as he followed his brother inside. "I'm coming in too, you know."

Troy glared at his brother, then hurried downstairs.

David went quietly to his room. Alan was already sleeping, so David sat on the edge of his bed and began removing his shoes in the dark.

"Did you have a good time?" Joanie Berringer whispered from the doorway.

"It was terrific. But I'm partial to water, remember?" He arose and walked to the door, glanced quickly at his sleeping brother, then joined his mother in the hall. "Alan's in bed early."

Joanie stopped and leaned her head against the wall. "He didn't have a good evening with you and Troy gone. I think he felt left out." She sighed deeply, her hand covering her tummy.

"You look wiped, Mom. Are you okay?"

"I think so. I just don't know what to do for Alan. He doesn't seem to try to handle his emotions at all. He just flings out in anger at the least little thing." Joanie closed her heavy eyelids over her weary eyes. "Maybe Troy can talk to him tomorrow." She straightened. "Where is Troy? Didn't he come home with you?"

"He's in his room. He kinda got put on the spot tonight...about Dad, so he's not too sociable right now."

"Maybe I'll go talk to him." She took a step toward the doorway. "O—oh!" Joanie doubled over in pain.

"Mom!" David grabbed his mother. "What is it?"

"I just need to go to bed," she said. David helped his mother to her bedroom.

"I'll go talk to Troy, Mom. You go to bed." David seated his mother on the bed.

"What did happen tonight?" Joanie asked wearily.

"One of the girls asked about Dad. He wouldn't talk to her. He just ran off."

Joanie sighed. "What happened then?"

"I told her about Dad, but I couldn't give her any details." He swallowed hard. "I just couldn't"

Joanie patted her son's hand. "It's okay. Someday it won't be so hard. Now off to bed you go. It's late and I need to sleep."

"Will you be all right? Can I get your medicine?"

"I'm okay and I've already taken my medicine. Don't worry."

David could hear Troy's tape deck as he headed down the stairs. The bedroom light was on, so David entered after knocking. Troy was seated, head in his hands, on the edge of his bed.

"Mom's sick again," David told him, before Troy could question his arrival. "The pains are back in her stomach."

Troy straightened, shaking his head slowly. "I wish she'd go to the doctor," he said. "She's had these pains for a long time."

David came to sit by Troy. "Do you think it's serious? C—could she die?"

Troy turned to David, startled at the comment. "Is she that sick?"

"She sure doesn't look good." David lowered his head,

his voice quiet. "I—I hope she doesn't die like Dad did."

Troy grabbed David's arm. "God wouldn't let that happen. It wouldn't be fair."

"I hope not," David whispered.

As if not hearing David's comment, Troy continued, "He couldn't. He wouldn't be God if he did."

David looked up at Troy, his eyes pleading. "I wish Alan wouldn't give her such a hard time. Mom's so worried about him. He had one of his tantrums tonight and now she seems sicker than usual."

Troy made for the door. "I'd like to shake that kid! Doesn't he know what he's doing to Mom?"

David grabbed Troy's sleeve. "Alan's sleeping and Mom's gone to bed, too. She said she just needed rest."

Troy went back to the tape deck and flipped over the cassette. "I'll sure talk to Alan tomorrow. He needs to know what he is doing to her."

"Something needs to be done," said David as he left the room. "Maybe he'll listen to you."

Troy flopped on the bed, letting the soothing music of Frank Mills soothe his anger at Alan and his concern about his mother.

Chapter Three

Two days after David's birthday in August, Troy got home from work to find the house unusually quiet. No supper smell welcomed him, no noise came from the television, and neither of his brothers announced his arrival.

"Anybody home?" Troy called into the empty hollowness. He walked up the stairs and into the kitchen. An uneasiness pulled at him. It was almost spooky. As he turned to leave the room, a note on the fridge caught his attention. He began reading even while lifting it from the magnetic clip: "Mom's sick. I've gone with her to the hospital. Alan is down the street at Johnson's. I'll call as soon as I know what is happening." The note was signed "David."

Troy tossed the paper onto the cupboard and headed back down the stairs. Flinging open the door, he came face to face with Shenade Johnson.

"Alan thought you'd be home now," Shenade said. Alan was standing behind Shenade.

"They took Mom in the ambulance!" Alan cried, stepping in front of Shenade. "She's gonna die! She's gonna die!" Shenade wrapped her arms around Alan to calm him.

Troy's mouth went dry, his knees weakened. "Who—?" The ring of the telephone interrupted. Troy scrambled to answer it. It was David.

"Mom's had a gall bladder attack, Troy. The doctor's given her something for pain and she seems better, but she wants to talk to you."

"W—where is she? Where are you?"

"We're at Call County Memorial. Bishop Schmidt will come for you. He's here."

"Call County?" Troy repeated.

"I'll give you a ride," Shenade said as she touched Troy's arm. He glanced at her, then, "We'll be right there. I have a ride."

"I'm coming too," Alan said before Troy could hang up.

Shenade grabbed Alan's hand and the three left the house. "Let's go get our car. Mom will let me use it." Shenade ran on ahead, pulling Alan right behind.

"Mom!" Shenade called, opening the heavy wooden door of her home. "Can I run Troy and Alan over to Call County? Their mother wants to talk to them."

Mrs. Johnson came from another room wiping her hands on her apron. "That'll be fine, Shenade," she said, and then to Troy, "You boys come for supper if your mother stays in the night, okay? You can tell me what is happening then."

Troy nodded, his "thank you" barely audible. He followed Shenade and Alan out the door.

Bishop Schmidt was standing with David when Troy and Alan entered their mother's hospital room. Shenade stayed in the doorway.

"Troy?" His mother's voice sounded tired. She held her hand out to him. Troy took it in his. Her face was white but calm, her eyelids heavy. "I guess I'm going to be here for a little while. The doctors want to remove my gall bladder first thing in the morning. This attack really interfered with my sugar levels so they want to operate as soon as possible. Do you think you boys can manage?"

Troy gulped hard, his eyes riveted to his mother's face.

"The boys will be fine, Mrs. Berringer," said Bishop Schmidt. "Don't you worry. You just get well." He rested his hand on Joanie's arm.

Troy nodded, giving his mother a weak smile.

"That's what I said too, Troy." David came to stand beside Troy. "We'll be okay."

Joanie Berringer looked for Alan. "You all take care of each other. I'll be home as soon as I can. Troy, you stay upstairs, sleep in my room until I return." Her eyelids closed for a long minute. Everyone stood silent. Slowly she opened them again. "I'm sorry about this, boys." Then her eyes closed again.

Bishop Schmidt motioned for the Berringer boys to follow him out of the room. Troy hesitated for a second, kissed his mother on the cheek, and left. Shenade moved aside but waited for Troy. They exchanged glances when he drew near, then sliding his hands into his pants pockets, he walked with her down the hall.

Bishop Schmidt stopped when they reached the lobby. "Did you drive down?" he asked Shenade.

"Yes. And I can take the boys home. Mom's invited them for supper."

"Good. Troy, do you think you can handle things at home or should I arrange for a housekeeper or sitter?"

"I—I..."

"We'll manage, Bishop," David put in. "I talked to Mom before she got the shot. There's food in the house and Troy knows where the grocery money is." David's eyebrows lifted. "I'll look after Alan and do the chores while Troy's at work. I'm sure we don't need a sitter." He looked anxiously at Troy. "Right, Troy?"

Troy didn't know what to think. Everything had happened so fast. In his mind he couldn't help but be fearful, an emotion he remembered all to clearly. "I—I think we can do it," he said softly.

David smiled widely. "Yeah, we can handle it."

Troy glanced at the bishop. "We'll give it a try."

"I'll be in touch with you boys every day and call the Relief Society to help out with some meals. I'll also be in to see your mother every evening."

"Can we come too, Bishop?" asked Alan. Troy noticed that Alan was holding on to Shenade's hand again.

"As soon as your mother is up to visitors," the bishop reassured. "You boys go with Shenade now and I'll call you later tonight."

They headed for the exit. "Oh, Troy," Bishop Schmidt hurried closer, "Dr. Johnson and I gave your mother a blessing just after she was admitted. I know she'll be okay."

"Thank you." Troy felt calmer, but the fear nagged at him. By the time they reached the car, Troy could feel a twinge of guilt. As they drove out of the parking lot the guilt had grown to anger. Troy felt as though he was abandoning his mother, leaving her behind. He felt helpless. Again images of his father under the tractor surfaced. The feeling of helplessness now was the same as it had been then.His fingers tightened into fists, his teeth clenched. How could God let this happen to his mother? To all of them? What if their mother died? Troy tried to shake the thoughts out of his head. She could die, the thought continued. Diabetics have complications lots of times. And surgery? Wasn't that risky in itself? Troy closed his eyes. But didn't Mom have a blessing? He tried to reassure himself. Oh, I don't know, he cried inwardly, it isn't fair.

A feathery touch on the back of his clenched fists made him open his eyes. "She'll be all right," Shenade said and then removed her hand.

Troy watched Shenade's small but deft hands on the steering wheel all the way to her house. Once the car was parked the boys followed her silently inside.

A foreboding silence struck Troy as the three boys entered their home two hours later. David went automatically to the television and turned it on. Stretching out on the floor, he quickly became absorbed in a weekly sitcom. Troy stood in the living room doorway not knowing what to do. Finally he went to the sofa and sat down. Immediately Alan was beside him. Troy was glad the television helped take his mind off the world around him. Even when Bishop Schmidt phoned to see if they needed anything, Troy was able to tell him not to worry. He went back to watching the program.

A little while later, Troy realized Alan's head was heavy on his arm. "Come on, Alan. It's time to go to bed."

"It's not my bedtime yet."

"It's past time." Troy led his brother down the hall to his bedroom. He rummaged through Alan's collection of baseball cards while his little brother undressed. "Don't forget your prayers," Troy said as Alan climbed into bed. Not waiting, Troy left the room.

The evening dragged and again the feeling of emptiness grew. Troy paced the floor, unable to settle into anything, so when David went to bed, Troy decided to follow. After getting his pajamas and tape deck, he went to his mother's bedroom. I can't sleep here, he thought. I feel as though I'm invading Mom's privacy. Remembering his mother's request, he shrugged and began to undress. A soft whimpering came from the doorway. He looked up to see his youngest brother.

"I—I—I'm scared," Alan said.

Troy held out his hand. "What are you scared of?"

"Is Mom going to die like Daddy did?" Troy gasped at Alan's question.

"Troy! Is Mom going to die?" he repeated.

Alan's body quivered. Troy pulled him close and wrapped his arm around him. Tears stung his eyes as he spoke. "No Alan, Mom's not going to die."

"How do you know?" he sobbed.

"She can't die, that's all." Troy tried to reassure himself as well as his brother. "We're going to ask Heavenly Father to help right now." The remark surprised Troy but he grabbed his little brother as he tried to pull away.

"What makes you think Heavenly Father will help this time?" Alan's voice was angry as he tugged against Troy's hold.

"I just know He will." Hearing himself say this was reassuring. "Let's get David. We can have family prayer together."

"He's sleeping," Alan said lessening his struggle.

"No, he's not," said a voice from the hall. "I can't sleep."

The relief at seeing David surprised Troy and he motioned for David to come. Tucking Alan between the two of them, they dropped to their knees. For a moment they remained silent, then Troy began: "H—Heavenly Father, please help us. Please don't let Mom die..."

Tears fell as fear and doubt surged briefly through him, then a feeling of calmness took over and he was able to offer a simple, sincere prayer.

Chapter Four

It was over a week now since Joanie's surgery. Bishop Schmidt had taken the boys to see their mother twice and Shenade drove them once. With the Relief Society bringing meals and doing laundry, the boys were coping well.

Troy hurried to work, leaving David and Alan lying on the living room floor watching Saturday morning cartoons. They reassured him they'd get the beds made, the vacuuming done and the dishes put away. He didn't need to worry.

Alan had awakened a little snippy this morning and Troy was leery about leaving. However, David said he could handle it. As Troy entered the store, he couldn't help feeling that something was about to happen.

"Morning," he said as he passed some of the other employees. He headed right out to the lumber yard, pushing his personal feelings to the back of his mind. Troy spent a lot of his working hours in the yard now, filling orders, writing invoices, and loading customers' vehicles.

Robert Matthew was already standing at the order desk with the ledger. "We need a fork lift driver this morning, Troy. Wanna tackle it?"

Troy's heart leapt and he felt a rising panic. "I—I..."

"Raynor Construction needs the half-inch plywood that

came in yesterday. Mr. Raynor is pulling his truck to the back."

Troy stood motionless. His feet were glued to the floor. He knew he should move but something held him back.

"You can manage the tractor, can't you?" Robert Matthews asked, taking in Troy's hesitancy.

Troy gulped. "Y—Yes," was barely a whisper.

"Mr. Raynor is waiting. The key is in the tractor."

Troy forced a step forward, then another. Robert Matthews went back to the paperwork he was doing. Troy walked stiffly outside. The yard was busy and he felt as though everyone was watching him. The fork lift was in its usual parking place.

"Hurry up, Berringer!" someone yelled. "Customer's waiting!"

Troy felt as though he were in a heavy cloudy mist. How could he ever get on that tractor? What if he overbalanced the load and the tractor flipped? He pictured himself lying on the dirty ground, fingernails digging into the earth. He felt suppressed. He couldn't breathe. He sucked in a gulp of air. I can't do this, he told himself, but when he took notice of his surroundings he was sitting on the seat, the black steering wheel staring at him.

His body was shaking; his cold and clammy hands dropped to his lap. He could see the key dangling. He ought to turn it. He could do this. A picture of his father passed through his mind again. He was conscious of the voices around him and the knot in his stomach.

"Troy? Can't you drive...Troy, are you all right?" Robert Matthews was standing next to the tractor. Now he climbed up next to Troy.

"I—I ca—" Troy could feel the anger begin to overpower the fear. His fists were tight on his lap, his teeth clenched. He felt the embarrassment redden his face.

"Troy?" Mr. Matthews placed a hand on Troy's

shoulder. Suddenly Robert Matthews remembered the bishop telling him about Troy's father and the accident, as well as Troy's part in it.

"You don't have to do this, Troy. Tom can drive."

"No," Troy said. "I—I can." He reached out to turn the key. He twisted it quickly and let go. The engine spurted and stopped. He turned the key hard this time, holding it longer than necessary. The starter growled, the motor started, then stopped.

"Just relax, Troy. It'll go."

Troy looked at his boss, at the tractor, and at those watching. His anger flared. His whole being was on fire. Jumping up, he leaped off the back of the tractor and ran out of the yard.

He ran and ran till he thought his chest would burst. He slowed to a walk. He had run almost all the way home. The physical exertion though, had calmed his anger. He felt so stupid. What would Mr. Matthews think of him now? He'd probably get fired for sure. Maybe I should go back, Troy told himself. Maybe I can explain. No. He stopped. What would I tell him? Stuffing his hands in his pockets, he walked slowly down the street. I'll just go home. Maybe Monday I can talk to him.

Troy was so busy thinking about the forklift and how he had panicked, he didn't hear the commotion until he had rounded the corner of the cresent.

"Alan! Open this door!"

Troy hesitated only a second, then sprinted.

"Alan, open this door or else!" David yelled. He was standing a few feet from the back door. A pounding came from inside the house. Then a crash.

Troy ran past David. He banged loudly on the door. "Alan! It's Troy. What are you doing?" Troy tried the doorknob. "Come on! Unlock the door!"

"No!" Alan screamed. "Go away!"

Troy turned to David. "What happened?"

"Who knows. One minute we were doing dishes, the next he was throwing stuff. I had to run outside to save my head. He got me once."

Troy could see the bruise already blue on David's cheek. "What'd he get you with?"

"The pancake turner, I think. When he picked up a table knife, I ran. He's really lost it this time." Another crash sounded against the door. "That's probably the last of his models," David told Troy.

Troy turned back to the door. "Alan! Open this door!"

"Go away. I wanna be alone!"

"You can be alone. Just let me in so we can get the work done before the Bishop comes." Troy tried to lower his voice.

There was a brief silence. "I don't want him to come anymore," came the trembling voice from inside.

"Why? He's only trying to help."

"Well, I don't want his help. I want my Da—"

Troy could hear Alan's voice crack. There was a muffled pounding and Troy could visualize Alan using his fists on the door.

"Please Alan," Troy spoke almost normal now. "Please let me in.

Troy and David waited. Finally the door opened a crack. Troy slowly pushed on it and went inside. He looked at the damage. Pieces of plastic toys, spoons, and other utensils were on the floor. Only one glass looked as though it had been smashed. Besides a couple of overturned chairs and the debris on the floor, everything else looked intact.

Troy was angry for an instant, then seeing Alan's pale face and red eyes he immediately crushed his anger.

"What's the matter?" he asked, facing Alan but not touching him. "Why the tantrum? You could have seriously hurt David."

"He shouldn't have said the things he did," Alan stuck

out his chin.

"What'd I say?" David asked, coming up behind Troy. "We were just doing the dishes."

"Yah! And saying how you liked living in town and goofing with the guys at church!" His voice was high-pitched now, nearly screaming. Wide-eyed he asked, "How can you say you like it here? You forgot Dad already?" He turned away.

David grabbed him. "Don't you think I miss Dad?"

"You didn't sound like it. You seemed happy to be here in this town."

David let go of his little brother. "I really miss Dad. Sometimes I even feel cheated that he left us. But I can't change what happened. All I can do is be grateful we're off the farm so I don't have to be reminded of it every day." His voice quivered and he looked away.

Alan dropped his head. "I didn't know."

Troy, too, was taken back with David's confession. He hadn't realized how deep David's feelings were. "Come on, guys. Let's get this stuff cleaned up. Alan, go get the broom and the dust pan."

Alan stood still looking at his shoes.

"Please?" Troy pleaded.

Alan turned slowly and headed for the kitchen. Troy started picking up the overturned chairs.

"What are you doing at home anyway?" asked David, suddenly realizing Troy should not be there.

Troy straightened. "I didn't have a good morning at work, so I came home."

David picked up some kitchen utensils. "Well, I'm sure glad you came when you did. I don't know what would have happened."

"Someday, he'll learn," Troy said.

"I hope he doesn't wait too long. I could lose my head."

The boys cleaned up the mess and Troy spent a few

minutes with Alan. "You just can't do that anymore. What would Mom think?"

Alan shrugged his shoulders. "I didn't think. I just got mad."

Funny, Troy thought. Alan had reacted the same way he had on the tractor this morning. Just the outcomes were different. Troy ruffled Alan's hair. "I guess we need to think before we fly off the handle. That kind of temper can get us into serious trouble. Dad used to tell me to go out behind the barn when I got angry and do push-ups. The more mad I was, the more push-ups I did. It sure worked when I did it."

"We don't have a barn," Alan snipped, not liking the reference to his father.

"Then come in here to your bedroom, or just stop where you are. Drop to the floor and start pumping and maybe you won't want to throw things or hit someone."

"Dad did that once, I remember," Alan cracked a grin.

Troy smiled. "Yeah, but he didn't do it often though. I only remember him actually doing it a couple times, and one of those was really funny."

Alan chuckled. "He was in his suit. I saw him."

"Yeah. He was so angry with someone or something. When he had done about fifty push-ups he said, "Well, I guess I'm humble enough to hear counsel now.""

"That was funny." This time Alan's smile was wide and his eyes glistened.

"See, Alan, Dad can still be with us in our memories. So please don't do this again."

"I'll try." He stopped then added, "I may be the most fit eleven year old around, 'cause I'll probably have to do hundreds of push-ups."

"Whatever it takes," Troy told him.

It was in church the next day as Troy listened half-heartedly to the High Council speaker that he began thinking about going to priesthood meeting and having to face Brother Matthews. However, he needn't have worried. Brother Matthews met Troy in the hall.

"Morning, Troy."

"Brother Matthews." Troy felt his cheeks go hot. Robert Matthews touched his fingers to Troy's arm. "I'm sorry about yesterday. It was unthinking of me to have you drive the tractor. I had forgotten."

"I've been thinking about that too," Troy said. "I'd like to try it again if I can. When no one's watching," he added.

"I'm sure we can arrange it. We'll watch for an opportunity." Robert Matthews gave Troy a reassuring smile.

"Thanks, Brother Matthews."

"It's all right, Troy." Robert Matthews hurried off. Troy watched him as he met his wife and teenage daughter, then left the building.

Chapter Five

Troy went with Bishop Schmidt to get his mother from the hospital the Sunday before school started. The Relief Society had come the day before to clean everything, fill the cookie jars and even cook Sunday dinner. It felt strange to walk downstairs at bedtime that night, but knowing his mother was in her room upstairs gave him a feeling of security and relief.

Tuesday morning Troy and his brothers started off to school. The sun was warm. Purple and white blossoms alternating with silver-grey shrubbery bordered the boulevard in front of their neighbor's house. In the yard, tall bronze marigolds and blue and burgundy columbines swayed in the breeze. Alan walked ahead, a light bounce in his step, his denim pack on his shoulders. He was beginning his last year in elementary school, finishing fifth grade; David was in his final year of middle school. As soon as they reached Griffin Consolidated, David and Alan waved good-bye to Troy. Waving back, Troy trudged the five blocks to Crestwood Heights, the only public high school in the district.

The school yard was teeming with busyness. Teens congregated in groups on the lawn, the sidewalks, and near the big double glass doors. Troy hesitated. He switched the jacket he carried from one shoulder to the other. I wish I had taken Shenade up on her offer, he told himself. On Sunday Shenade had suggested driving him to school this morning but he had declined. He didn't want to be chauffeured by a girl his first day. Now he wished he were not alone.

Troy entered the school and knew instantly that his life was going to be totally different than what he had been used to other years. This was a beehive. Students milled everywhere: coming, going, talking, laughing. The school he attended last year had been busy on the first day, but nothing like this. Rossland had 150 students, here there were that many right in the hallway, and three times that number still outside.

Troy stood eyeing everything and everyone around him. The display case on the opposite wall was full of trophies and awards. Pictures of youths holding medallions and plaques lined the back. Straightening his shoulders, Troy pushed himself through the throng of bodies until he reached the office window. The secretary pointed him towards his locker and homeroom. Even her kindly smile didn't dispel his anxiety. He never once saw anyone vaguely familiar, not even Kristin or Shenade.

Troy spent the morning working out his course schedule. Several times he made trips to the office to rearrange classes. As he walked home at noon his head was spinning.

"How did it work out?" Joanie asked from the sofa where she was lying when he came home at noon. Troy tossed his jacket down, covering his mother's toes that peeped from under her pink brushed nylon lounger.

"I can't do this, Mom," Troy's voice was firm. Everything's different. I can't even take the classes I need to graduate."

"I don't understand. This is such a large school." She pulled herself to sit up.

"There are lots of options for me to take to get my credits, but the ones I want are full in the time slots I need them. Because there are so many students, I can't rearrange the academic courses in any way to allow me to take the automotive mechanics and woodwork I wanted to continue from last year."

"What will you do? Take another semester?"

"You wanna see?" Troy took his schedule sheet out of his pants pocket and handed it to his mother. "Here, have a look." He slumped into the armchair, giving his mother time to look at the paper. "Funny, eh? Can you picture me taking drama?" He paused. "Me!" His voice grew louder. "And to top that embarrassment, I have to take a course by correspondence to get the credits I need." Troy smacked the arm of the chair with his fist. "It's not fair!"

Jumping to his feet he hurried to the dining room. While Joanie still looked at the schedule, Troy sent a cacophony of aggressive notes through the house. His fingers pounded the keys so hard, the house shook. Joanie ignored the noise for a few minutes then gingerly started for the dining room. Before she could get to Troy, the outside door slammed.

"Troy's at it again!" called David as he took the stairs two at a time. Alan was right behind him.

Immediately Troy stopped playing. His face first reddened, then fell when he turned to see his mother almost at his side. David threw his backpack on the table.

"Hello, boys," Joanie greeted.

Troy turned to face David. "How did you make out with courses?"

"Not bad." He pulled his schedule from his pack and tossed the crumpled paper to Troy. "I had to change some things but I don't mind. I took classes that had my friends in."

"That figures." Troy gave the paper to his mother. "I don't know one person in any of the classes I previewed this morning."

"It's only a half day today," David said, "Maybe tomorrow."

"I only know the two girls from the Sunday School class. I don't think there's much chance of seeing them."

"And you couldn't take any other options, eh?" Joanie was beside him now, his schedule still in her hand.

"Nope, we tried everything. I'll have to take what I've scheduled—this semester anyway." The knot in his stomach tightened.

"We have lots of kids in sixth grade." Alan was finally able to speak. "And we don't have any fifth grade kids with us. One grade in each class!"

Troy was playing the piano again and didn't hear the exchange between Alan and his mother. All Troy could do was disappear into his music, burying all his frustrations: the new school, the fork lift he still hadn't driven, and his role as the oldest son-cum-father in the family. Life sure wasn't fair.

Troy walked alone to school again the second day. He was more familiar with where he was going and some of the beehive activity was gone, so he headed down the hall toward his locker. Stuffing the books inside, Troy slammed the door shut and shuffled off to his homeroom for attendance check.

The classes of the day seemed long but Troy enjoyed most academic subjects—math and chemistry being his specialties. He wished he didn't have to take that stupid drama. It was such a dumb thing for a guy to do.

Troy headed for the fine arts room the last period of the day. He entered to find a commotion between two boys on the stage. A large group of other students were watching and cheering from the sidelines. The teacher, Mr. Stephen MacDonald, referred to by everyone as Mr. Mac, entered the room just ahead of Troy.

"Don't waste your talents, Sammy boy. You'll have lots of opportunities to express yourself when we start the play."

"We were showing Pam and Carol how we simulate fights! We were good, weren't we?" Sam Livingston, a peaked looking teen with long dangly arms, took a playful swing in the air. "Are we going to do a play like the one we did last year?"

"There's lots to choose from, but I do have some preferences." Mr. Mac stood in front of the handful of students who now seated themselves on the edge of the stage. Troy remained standing to one side. Being here was so dumb. These kids looked like dorks.

"He's only frightening for the first day," came a husky whisper over Troy's shoulder. Troy grinned at the tall dark youth behind him.

"Bob! We wondered if you were going to grace this class with your presence." The teacher ambled over to Troy and Bob.

"I wouldn't miss it, Mr. Mac. You know I need your staid personality to keep me sober through the other classes."

The students laughed at the apparent sarcasm and Troy wondered why this jock-looking type was in a drama class.

For the next eighty minutes he found out. Bob might look like a football player, he might even be one, but he sure had the respect of the class. Troy liked him immediately as he did Sammy Livingston, who turned out to be the class clown. He was also happy to see Kristin and Shenade there. They were at least someone he knew.

At the end of the class Troy left with the others. It was then he noticed for the first time the white sheet that was draped over a piece of furniture. He hesitated briefly as he felt a surge of adrenalin, then went over and lifted one corner. As soon as he saw the baby grand piano he wanted to play it.

"It's a beauty, isn't it?" Mr. Mac said as he pulled the cover off the piano. After opening the keyboard he plunked a couple of keys. "I wish I could play," he said. "But I don't." Turning to Troy he asked, "Do you?"

"A little." Troy blushed.

"Try it." Mr. Mac stepped aside.

"No," Troy shook his head but his fingers touched the cool keys and with one hand tapped out a few notes.

"It's here anytime you want to play it," Mr. Mac smiled. "Except when there's a class."

Troy smiled slightly and nodded. Mr. Mac re-covered the piano and they left the room together.

"Does he always have to play the piano?" David asked from the kitchen later that evening.

"The piano has priority over T.V. Remember?" Joanie said as she hung up the tea towel. "Anyway, you have homework to finish."

"I finished before supper and it's too windy to go outside."

"Can't you read or play games with Alan or something?" After shutting off the kitchen light they went into the living room. Alan lay on his stomach on the floor doing word puzzles in a tattered book. He looked up at the mention of his name.

"Nah!" David snickered and sat on Alan's back. "He's a squirt."

"Who's a squirt?" Alan protested the weight, twisting and turning to throw off his assailant.

"Not me," teased David, and Alan squealed as David grabbed him and began tickling him.

"Boys! David!" Joanie scolded after a minute. "That's enough, something will get broken."

The boys continued for a moment longer, then when Troy banged the keys of the piano they stopped.

"Come on," invited David. "Let's play Scotland Yard."

"I'll be the bad guy," Alan hollered as he ran to the closet to get the board game.

"You wanna play?" David asked Troy when he stuck his

head around the corner.

"Sure, why not?" Troy replied.

"I'll pop some popcorn," Joanie smiled affectionately at Troy. "Then I'm going to soak in a hot tub."

Soon the boys were engrossed in a board game of search and evasion. Joanie's heart warmed as she placed the large bowl of popcorn in front of the three boys. She watched them play for a few minutes then happily made her way to the bathroom.

"Alan and David went to their room," Troy told his mother sometime later. "I'll be in mine doing homework if you need me."

"Thank you, Troy." Joanie gave her oldest son a brief hug. "I'm off to bed right now. I've had a busy day."

"Can I help in some way?"

"Not right now. I have a few things to think about financially, then I'll probably ask you for advice."

"Me?"

"You're old enough to help me make some decisions, but not tonight, I'm just too tired."

"Okay, I'll help if I can." Troy started to walk away, then turned back. "Thanks for the popcorn."

"Thank you for playing with the boys."

"It was fun." Troy went downstairs and turned on his tape deck. Simon and Garfunkel's album, "Sounds of Silence," played while he finished up his school assignments.

Troy glanced around at the people sitting in the congregation as he entered the chapel on Sunday. With his hands stuffed in his pants pockets, he slid on to the bench where he usually sat with his mother.

"Good morning, Troy." Bishop Schmidt approached him with an outstretched hand. Troy shook it.

"Hi," he said with reservation.

"I'd like to invite you to bless the sacrament this

morning," the bishop said.

"I'd rather not," Troy's chin dropped.

"I think—," the bishop started, then hesitated. "Maybe next time," he said.

Troy kept his head bowed right through the opening song. He raised it only after opening prayer had been said and the man who had said it had taken a seat at the sacrament table with the Elder's Quorum president and Troy's boss, Robert Matthews.

Troy couldn't wait to escape when the meeting was over. He was glad that the sun was warmer today. The trees surrounding the parking lot were an ornate orange and gold and brown. Troy inhaled the damp-wooden smell of autumn. He ignored the voices behind him and walked the whole perimeter of the parking area before returning to the building. After a stop in the bathroom to comb his sandy colored hair, he went to priesthood meeting. Somehow he didn't mind attending this class. There were no priests in the ward but him, and because he would be eighteen in May, Mr. Matthews had invited him to attend with the elders.

Troy listened intently to the lesson on the plan of salvation and was grateful that his parents had been married for eternity in the temple. He felt reassured when Mr. Matthews talked about a husband and wife being sealed by the Holy Spirit of Promise. Somehow he knew that his parents were recipients of that divine sealing. Troy gulped hard when images surfaced of his father in the casket and under the overturned tractor. He shook them away. I'm not going to cry, he thought. He looked around to see if anyone had heard his thoughts, but everyone's attention was on the teacher. I wish I didn't think about the accident and funeral all the time. Troy closed his eyes, trying to shut everything out, and was glad when the closing prayer was said. He didn't wait for his family when services were over, but walked alone the short distance home.

Troy eyed the piano all through dinner and was not pleased when his mother reminded him that it was his turn to help her do the Sunday dishes. Joanie caught Troy's disappointed look and said, "Why don't you begin washing while I clear off the table, then I'll dry. That way you'll get done sooner."

"You hate drying," Troy said, his hands full of silverware.

"I really don't mind. So scoot."

Troy sank his hands into the hot soapy water all ready in the sink. He chuckled to himself as he heard his mother coax Alan to eat his unwanted peaches. "Some things never change," Troy said aloud.

"What doesn't change?" asked Joanie.

Troy smiled. "Oh, the way you get us to eat fruit and vegetables."

"I get better with practice. Haven't you noticed?" Joanie held up a glass she was drying.

"Was I as hard to deal with as Alan is?"

"Sometimes," Joanie answered, putting the glass on the shelf. "But if kids were perfect all the time, where is a parent's challenge?"

"Don't you think you've had your share of challenges?"

"Yes, but there are blessings that come from enduring."

"I suppose. Giving yourself needles twice a day can't be fun, though."

"No, but at least there is help for diabetes. It's not like having a disease that can't be treated."

"That may be true," Troy said wiping his hands on his mother's tea towel, "but how does a person learn to endure? The thought of giving myself a needle once a day would do me in." Troy waited until his mother had put the last kettle in the cupboard.

Joanie placed a hand on Troy's shoulder. "Remember the saying about persisting? The more we do something, the easier it becomes. It's not the task that becomes easier, it's our ability that increases."

"And that pertains to you?"

She dropped her arm. "I didn't always accept the diabetes, but when I quit fearing the disease and the needles it became easier. I couldn't make them disappear, so I learned to accept them for the help they were." Her voice quivered slightly. "It was difficult, and sometimes it still is, but the Lord has helped me there. I had to change my attitude and trust in Him to help me."

Troy didn't say anymore. He just wished he was strong like his mother. Oh, he was helping with Alan and the push-up suggestion was working. He had come across his little brother several times down on the floor huffing and puffing as he pumped. Troy would give him the high sign and smile. However, he still wasn't driving the fork lift. Mr. Matthews had left that decision to Troy. "When you're ready," he had said. "There are lots of other things you can do."

Troy reminded himself he had to start reading Shakespeare's *Macbeth* for English and that reminded him of drama, and that made him mad. Drama was for sissies. He couldn't figure out why some kids were in that class. It was such a loser course and they weren't. He decided to go for a walk. He'd read later.

The midafternoon sun was warmer than usual for this time of year, so Troy just flipped his sweater over his shoulder and held it with one finger. His other hand auto-matically went into his pants pocket. A magpie squawked from a nearby tree and the neighbor's dog barked as Troy passed their yard. The park was surrounded by evergreens, red ash, and brown and gold poplar, secluding it from the busy streets. Troy lingered, breathing in the autumn aroma. This was one of his father's favorite seasons. Harvest was completed, the colors around the farm brilliant, and the autumn smells—oh, how his father loved them. He gulped down a lump.

A movement out of the corner of his eye made Troy turn. Across an open area of grass was Shenade Johnson, perched on an oversized wooden stile that straddled a small irrigation ditch, a white pad and pencil in her hand. Her pastel colored outfit and sandy-blonde hair made her look like springtime. He approached her cautiously, pushing the former thoughts to the back of his mind. "Hi," he said.

With a start she looked up. "Hi." Her reply was cheery.

"At it again, I see." He flushed slightly.

"It's necessary today, though. I have an assignment for art class."

"May I see?" Troy stretched to make himself taller to look over the edge of the art pad.

"I'm not done yet." Shenade's face reddened. She held the project closer to her and Troy backed away. Shenade looked first at Troy, then at her paper. Slowly she lowered it.

"That's fantastic!" He stood by her side to look at it right side up. "You're good. Where did you ever learn to draw like that?"

"I don't know. I just do it."

"I'm impressed." His eyes met hers briefly. "I'll let you get back to your work," he said after a moment and started to leave.

"Will I see you at the fireside tonight?" Shenade asked hurriedly.

"Oh, yeah, I forgot. 7:00, right?"

"Yes, we're going to watch a new video that's out."

"Do you know what it is?"

"It belongs to Mrs. Peterson. Something about a guardian angel or miracles or something."

"I sure hope it's not dumb."

"Me too." Shenade's attention returned to her paper. Troy paused for a moment to watch her, then turned away.

The church foyer was bustling with people when the Berringer boys entered the church. The couches, sofas, and chairs were pulled away from the walls and throw cushions were on the floor. The video machine was set up and ready to go.

"I'd like all of you to find a place to sit so we can start," Mrs. Johnson announced.

After a minute of hustle and confusion, the bishop stood beside Mrs. Johnson and immediately the room grew silent. Troy found himself seated by Shenade and Kristin on the sofa. After a brief explanation the bishop started the video.

The overture at the beginning stopped Troy short. "It's A Miracle." This was one of his father's favorite plays and he loved to sing the songs. Troy wasn't sure if he could sit through this. He glanced at David. He had his head down, his hands holding his chin. He, too, was struggling with the memories, thought Troy. Tears threatened and the anger flared when the father in the movie began to sing "In the Hollow of Thy Hand."

"I'll sing that song at your missionary farewells," his father had kept telling his sons. Now that would never happen.

As soon as the movie was over, Troy fled. Neither he nor David stayed for lunch. Running all the way home, Troy escaped to his room where he could cry openly.

Chapter Six

"Alan, I want you to go to school. You're late already." Joanie stood above her youngest son who was sitting on the step, lazily tying his shoes.

"I'll go when I'm ready."

"I'd like you to be on time more than just when it suits you."

"I'm going, aren't I? You should be happy about that." Alan stomped dirt off his shoes onto the dingy carpet as he left the house.

One of these days...Joanie thought as she stood unmoving. Taking a deep breath to calm her anger, she stated aloud, "I wish I knew what to do with him." As she worked through her morning chores, Joanie tried to think of ways to deal with Alan. So far, Troy was her best solution. Alan would listen and respond to him, but right now Troy seemed to be having his own problems. In her heart Joanie kept a fervent prayer that something would help her deal with Alan.

For Troy, the day didn't go well at all. Mr. Friemont gave a spot quiz in English and Troy failed it. Besides all that, he had forgotten his lunch at home, so his irritability snowballed. By the time drama class came around, his negative attitude stood out like neon lights.

"Girl problems?" chided Sam before class started. Troy glared at him. "Don't cross Berringer's path today, guys. His looks could kill."

"Park it!" Troy dropped his duffle bag on a chair.

"Okay, okay," called Mr. Mac from behind the backdrop. "Troy, come on up and finish painting this brick wall. Sam! Sand boxes."

Troy jumped onto the stage in one leap, but scraped the calf of his leg on the way up. He would have sworn had Carol and Pam not been right there painting windows on the side wall. They giggled as he disappeared behind the wooden backdrop.

"I've done the red," Mr. Mac told him. "You take the black and go over the pencil lines to emphasize the brick look."

Troy reached for the can of black paint Mr. Mac was holding. Another smart remark from Sam made him turn away, so when Mr. Mac let go of the open can, Troy did not have a good grasp on it. With a sickening thud, the full can hit the floor spurting black paint on Troy's new pants, on Mr. Mac's blue cords and big blobs all over the red backdrop.

Troy's mouth dropped open. He stared at Mr. Mac. The teacher gazed in disbelief at the backdrop and then at his pants. Troy hoped the stage would open up and swallow him. Even Sam was quiet. Finally the drama teacher spoke. "Do you work tonight?" he asked firmly.

Troy could only shake his head.

"I'll be marking papers. Meet me at seven thirty and you can spend a couple of hours fixing up this unnecessary mishap."

Troy nodded and they both left to clean up.

Troy did not return to class. He walked in the cool fall breeze all the way home. His mother questioned him when he entered the house earlier than usual, "Troy, is something wrong? Are you sick?"

"Only in the head," he muttered to himself from the closet as he hung up his coat. Joanie was there when he turned around. "Does paint come out of denim?" He looked down at his pants, his mother's gaze following his. "Please don't ask," he told her.

"Take them off and I'll soak them. If it's latex paint it may come out. I'll see what I can do." Joanie resisted the urge to ask him what happened. She realized that would only make matters worse.

"I have to go back to school at seven thirty to do some painting. I hope that doesn't mess up home evening."

"We'll have it at the supper table."

"Thanks," he said and went down the stairs.

A subdued atmosphere in the Berringer house carried over through supper. Even Joanie seemed preoccupied. As soon as they had eaten, she began talking to the boys.

"I don't have a lesson as such tonight, but I have some business I think we should discuss as a family." Her voice was solemn. "I'll talk and then you can ask questions. All right?"

All three nodded. Troy watched as his mother's shaking hands drew some papers out of the pocket of her apron. They were filled with numbers and figures. She explained how their father's affairs were all settled and all the bills paid. The home they were in and their small second hand car were paid off, but the cash flow was gone. David and Alan looked at each other, not really comprehending what they heard. Troy stared at his mother. "What will we do?"

"We've made what little money we had stretch a long way, but now it's gone. I've talked to the bishop and to a counsellor from Family Support Services." Troy dreaded what was coming next. "I was counselled to go on social assistance for right now." Troy shook his head. More wonderful things to make him feel good. His mother continued, "My health is slow in returning, but as soon as I am better, I'll try to go back to teaching elementary school." Troy knew she had taught school until she started having children.

The boys looked at each other. Joanie continued, "I need to know how you feel about this, Troy."

"I guess we don't have any other choice, do we?" There was no sarcasm in his voice. "I'll try to make my money take care of my needs and I could help buy a few groceries."

"And with the paper route I can help too," David volunteered.

"And Alan and I will do what we can. It's only temporary. Hopefully by next school term I'll be able to teach at least part-time."

"I'll be working full time as soon as I graduate," Troy added. "Then I can pay some room and board."

"So, we'll make it," said Joanie positively. "We just have to work together. Let's have family prayer before Troy has to go back to school."

The four Berringer's knelt around the table and David took his turn to pray. "Thank you, Heavenly Father, for our many wonderful blessings—" Troy wondered what their blessings were.

He hurried in the cool night air. For some reason, after family prayer Troy didn't feel depressed. He should be. His mother had just dropped a bombshell on him, and now he was running off to school to repair damage he had caused? Why wasn't he miserable? Troy slowed his pace as he headed into the north wind. It didn't make sense. As he walked, oblivious to the nip in the air, the feeling of well-being stayed with him.

The school looked dark and ominous, but the door opened when Troy tried it. The halls echoed a foreboding hollowness with each footstep on the polished tiles. Finally, he rounded a corner to find the next hallway lit. Voices came from the fine arts room and Troy followed them.

"Here he comes." Sam Livingston spotted Troy first.

Ignoring Troy's questioning look, Sam continued with a twinkle in his eye. "I feel partly responsible for the mess this afternoon, so I'm here to make amends." He held up a can of red paint for Troy to see.

Shenade and Bob stuck their heads out from around the backdrop. "And we had to come and make sure he does," Bob said, handing Troy the can of black paint. "Here, you can help Shenade finish. I'm going to help Kristin get the pizza."

Troy took the open paint can, but didn't move until Bob was out of the room. "Pizza?" He moved to where Shenade was waiting with a small paint brush.

"We're sharing the paint," she informed him.

"Oh!" He held it out for her to dip her brush in.

"We pitched in for a pizza and root beer," Sam said. "I work better with food." He knelt on the floor near some paper and put the lid on his red paint.

"Are you finished?" Shenade asked him.

"Don't see any black blobs now, do you?" Sam gestured toward the red wall.

"No," Troy said, seeing no evidence of the splatters.

"See, I can do a good job. Now I wonder where the pizza is?" He looked toward the closed door. "Those two probably got sidetracked." Sam jumped off the stage. "I'd better go check on them."

"What made you guys come and help? I was the one who made the mess." Troy stopped painting the black pencilled lines and looked directly at Shenade.

She rose from her kneeling position. "It was Bob's idea."

"I don't understand."

"Bob's a pretty neat guy. Weird sometimes, but neat just the same. He's the one who told Sam you didn't need any more hassle and that he had acted like a jerk."

"A real jerk!" pouted Sam, jumping back onto the stage. "My mouth gets in gear before my brain."

"I understand," said Troy. "My emotions seem to rule

mine."

"Friends, then?" Sam asked.

Troy nodded with a grin, then went back to painting.

"How do you manage to be out on a home evening night?" Troy asked Shenade when they were alone behind the backdrop.

"Our home evenings are flexible. My dad's a doctor, so the weeks he's on call on Monday we hold home evening on Sunday."

"I'm glad you're here," he said, painting another black line.

"Me, too." Shenade dipped her brush into the paint. They looked at each other for a brief moment, the color rising in their cheeks. Troy was the first to look away.

Soon the job was done and the five high school kids proudly eyed their work. An empty pizza box lay discarded on the floor, pop cans strewn around it.

"We'll clean up if you'll play the piano," Shenade said to Bob.

Troy looked at Bob in surprise. What other talents did this guy have? he wondered.

"Are you sure?" Bob glanced at Kristin and the other two boys in turn.

"Yeah," bubbled Kristin, already picking up the debris.

As soon as the music began to fill the room, Troy found himself drawn to the baby grand and he just wanted to play those ivory keys. He stood behind Bob and watched the youth's fingers move on the keyboard.

"Play Joe Cocker's new one," Kristin spoke as soon as she reached them.

"Is the work all done?" Mr. Mac asked as he waddled into the room, his chubby legs dragging under his massive bulk.

"This is the last load!" Sam called. "So keep playing!"

Bob tried but finally gave up when his rendition was full

of more wrong notes than right ones. Troy leaned over and with one finger plunked out a few notes of the melody.

"Do you play?" Bob asked. It was his turn to look surprised.

"Some."

"Can you play "On The Edge Of A Dream"? Kristin excitedly pulled Bob from the bench.

Troy looked at the kids, then at the piano. Was his fear greater than his desire to sit at that beautiful instrument? he asked himself, his eyes meeting Sam's, then Bob's, and then Shenade's.

"Go ahead," Shenade smiled at him.

Troy sat at the piano. The keys felt cold, his fingers stiff. The tune began very choppily, but soon it flowed through the room.

"Lift the top!" Mr. Mac stepped up to the piano. Troy stopped playing, a sudden redness covering his face. "Lift the top," Mr. Mac repeated, "and get the full effect."

Bob propped open the top and Troy resumed playing. The tone was resonant and Troy loved the full sound. His fingers danced over the keys, playing the notes as he remembered them.From one song to another he played—songs the teens asked for. At one point, when he hesitated, Mr. Mac suggested it was getting late.

"Just one more," Sam insisted. "A duet, maybe?"

"Chopsticks!" Shenade suggested and Bob slid back onto the bench.

The two boys played hard and fast until they were all laughing so much they couldn't keep their fingers going.

"A good place to stop," Mr. Mac informed them with a smile. "It's after ten. My wife will shoot me."

"You don't have a wife!" Sam laughed.

"Well, she'd shoot me if I had one." Mr. Mac helped Troy put the cover on the piano. "And your mothers will probably shoot you.

"Come on, I'll give you three a ride home," Mr. Mac said to Sam, Kristin and Shenade. "Can I offer you one too, Troy?"

"Troy lives close to me," Shenade said, glancing quickly at Troy.

"You're driving me home, aren't you, Big Bobby?" Kristin grabbed Bob's arm with both hands. "You promised, remember?"

Bob took her hand and headed across the grass once they were outside. "See you tomorrow," he hollered over his shoulder.

Mr. Mac stopped in front of the Johnson home and Shenade got out. "I'll take you home," Mr. Mac told Troy when he followed Shenade.

"I'll walk from here, thanks. I only live around the corner."

"Go right home," Sam teased.

Troy grinned and shut the door, then he turned to Shenade. "I appreciate all your help tonight."

"It was fun. I enjoyed it." Shenade started up the sidewalk.

Unwilling to have the evening end so soon, Troy asked, "Where did you get a name like Shenade? I've never heard it before. Is it a family name?" Troy's flushed face remained hidden in the darkness.

Shenade paused at her door. "My mom has a thing for unusual names. I'm not sure where she heard it. Someday I'll ask her."

"Well, I'd better go," Troy said, not knowing what else to say. "It's getting late." Troy still hesitated. "Shenade?" It was almost a whisper.

"Yes?"

"I like your name." He left then without waiting to see the girl's smile.

"Troy?" Joanie called when he opened his front door.

"Hi, Mom."

"How did it go?" She came to the top of the stairs.

"Fine," he said, amazed that it had. "Real fine." As he went down the stairs he added, "I love you, Mom."

Chapter Seven

Paul Arnett, the new Young Men's president, welcomed Troy and David to the youth activity when they arrived at the church on Tuesday. "Sister Johnson will give you each a colored card when you enter the gym. Our activity will be in there tonight."

"I forgot the guys were in charge this month," David said. "We planned this neat game at our meeting last week."

"Oh, this should be fun." Troy wasn't impressed. "It's probably charades or some dumb thing like that."

"Yeah, some dumb thing like that," David returned lightly. "But you'll like it."

"Oh, sure. About as much as a cat likes getting wet."

"Yes," David looked directly at Troy. "They only get wet if there's a reason."

"Well, I don't have a reason."

"You don't need one, you're not a cat." David smacked Troy playfully on the arm. "C'mon!" Together the two boys walked into the large gym.

The kids, already there, were chatting, comparing colored cards. "Here, boys," Sister Johnson handed a blue card to David, a yellow one to Troy, once she had greeted them. "Take a chair in your particular color group. That will be your team."

Troy found himself sitting with four of the youngest youths, two boys and two girls. He looked over at David, who was carrying on a conversation with Shenade, a blue card in her hand also. Figures, Troy thought.

Just then Kristin entered with her usual bustling flare. Troy watched her bounce over to Sister Johnson, grab a card and come towards him. "Oh, good, you're yellow too." Kristin slid a chair closer to Troy. "We'll show that blue team, won't we?"

Troy couldn't help feeling better. "We'll try," he told her. "I'm glad you're on my team. I was beginning to feel a little childish." He motioned to the other yellow team members.

"I see what you mean."

Paul Arnett welcomed everyone to the activity. "Troy, can I get you to say opening prayer?"

Troy was about to decline but, upon receiving a jab from Kristin, rose and gave the prayer. She grinned as he returned to his chair.

The activity turned out to be more fun than Troy expected. The yellow and blue teams played paper charades, drawing clues instead of acting them out. Some of the advisors even took part and Troy enjoyed that.

When the evening was over Troy found himself helping in the kitchen. He didn't even mind washing the banana split dishes while two of the younger girls dried. The laughter and joviality of the evening was contagious.

Just as they finished the dishes, Sister Johnson entered the kitchen, Shenade on her heels. "I'm not going right home, Shenade. I have a young women's board meeting at 8:45."

"Can I take the car?" Troy heard Shenade ask.

"I'd rather you didn't. I have to drop Sister Shaw off after and I do have a load to take."

Troy left the kitchen before the Johnson's conversation ended. Halfway across the hall he heard his name called.

When he turned around he saw Shenade coming toward him with her arms full. "I told Mom I'd load the car for her. Would you mind helping me put the two easels in the back of our station wagon?"

"Sure," Troy replied and went to pick one up.

"I'm going home, Troy!" David called from the gym door.

"Come and take one of these on your way out, okay?"

David took an easel and followed Troy to the car. "Is there more stuff to bring?" Troy asked Shenade.

"Just a couple of boxes, but I can get them."

"I don't mind helping." Troy followed her into the church after saying good-bye to David.

When they reached the car again Troy asked, "Are you walking or are you waiting for your Mom?"

"I have studying to do, so I'd better get home. Midterms are coming fast."

"Don't I know it. I've never worked so hard to get good grades."

Together they started across the parking lot. "Was your school very different from Crestwood?" Shenade asked.

"We didn't have semesters so our classes weren't more than forty minutes long. And we took all our subjects all year."

"I don't know if I'd like it that way. You'd have to remember everything for ten months, and you have six or eight subjects at once. To me that seems harder."

"I suppose the semester system is better. I guess I'm just used to the other way." Troy's voice quivered. "There's lots of things I've had to change."

Shenade noticed the small quiver. "I bet it is hard. I don't know if I could do it."

"You probably could if you had to."

"Maybe," Shenade said, "but I hope I never have to."

"I hope you don't either." Troy smiled at Shenade in the

darkness.

The late fall wind met them face to face as they rounded the corner at the end of their crescent. Both of them hugged their jackets tighter. After a lengthy silence, Shenade spoke. "October is the Young Women's turn to plan the activity. Our class wants a Halloween party, you know, spook alley and dance or something. Mom thought it was a neat idea, so on Sunday we'll discuss it in Bishop's Youth Committee meeting."

Troy, glad that Shenade had changed the subject, breathed easier. "That could be fun." he answered. "We had neat spook alleys in Rossland,"

Shenade stopped walking. "You did! Would you help us? We've never tried it here before."

Troy's hesitation was not due to a lack of response. He couldn't take his eyes away from Shenade's face that shone under the street light. She turned and continued walking.

"I'd like that," he told her and hurried to walk beside her. "My mom and dad—" he swallowed hard but continued, "my mom and dad were fabulous last year at Halloween. They were in charge of a surprise spook alley for our ward. You should have seen it. They found this old derelict house and turned it into a superb fright night."

They stopped in front of Shenade's house. "Would you help us?"

"Sure. It could be fun," Troy said opening the gate for her.

She entered her yard but turned before opening the door. "I'm glad you're here, Troy," she said hurriedly then scurried inside. Troy's step was light as he walked home, glancing back over his shoulder several times. When he got home, the house was quiet. A note lay on the top step. "Troy," his mother had written, "I have a meeting with the bishop at 9:15. Alan and David are in their room. I hope you had a good time. Good night, Mom." Troy smiled at the note. Finding a pencil in a kitchen drawer he added a few lines to the paper and left it on the stairs before going to his room.

After turning on his Montavani tape, he lay on the bed and stared up at the ceiling. He thought of the evening's activity and the variety of emotions that he had experienced. First, there was the fear when he had to say the prayer, then the fun he had playing with Kristin and the others on the yellow team. Then there were feelings he had when he found himself being carried away with Shenade's absorbing eyes, and the hollow empty feeling of separation when he mentioned his father. Yet he had spoken about him as if he were still alive. Sometimes, Troy admitted, his father felt really close. The familiar tightness once again grew in his chest. When will it stop hurting? "Please help me," Troy heard himself say aloud, knowing that one of his fathers in heaven would hear. He felt his body relax and he must have dozed. The shutting of the outside door awakened him and he heard his mother pause halfway up the stairs. Troy sat up, realizing his mother must be reading his note: "Mom, I had a good time. I love you, Troy."

He heard his mother walk into the kitchen and then to her bedroom. Troy glanced at the clock-radio on his night-stand. It was 10:20. I did doze off, Troy thought as he grabbed his chemistry book to read over some formulas.

"I have to work after school tonight," Troy told his mother the next morning as he tied his shoes at the bottom of the stairs. We have a pre-Christmas shipment coming in. I'll be home about 5:30."

Before she could speak, David darted down the hall and onto the top step. "I'll beat you this morning," Troy challenged and both boys left the house in a rumble of noise, slamming the door behind them. Joanie smiled contentedly as she turned toward the kitchen to tidy up the breakfast dishes.

October was turning out to be a busy month. With the Halloween party and a drama competition before Christmas, Troy found himself far more occupied than usual. Sundays seemed to be the only day to slow down.

When Troy left priesthood meeting the second Sunday, he could see his mother visiting with Betty Jean Johnson. Since she had just been sustained as a girl's youth advisor, he figured she'd be awhile. Zipping his jacket, he made for the chapel door. His mind was miles away, his eyes focused on the blowing trees around the parking lot.

"Troy?" a hand clasped his shoulder, and he recognized the bishop's voice. "May I speak to you for a few minutes?"

Troy didn't like the sound of this. "I suppose," he said pushing his fists deep into his pockets.

"Let's go into my office. Then we won't be disturbed." Troy followed Bishop Schmidt down the windowless hallway, dragging his feet all the way. Once in the office Troy stood with his back to the closed door while the bishop took his place behind the desk. "I like to start every discussion, no matter how informal, with a word of prayer. Would you join me?"

Troy watched the bishop kneel at his desk and shyly followed. His busy mind couldn't focus clearly on the words Bishop Schmidt spoke, but he did feel the warmth of the spirit the man radiated. "Amen," repeated Troy automatically as he arose from his knees.

"Have a chair, Troy."

Troy sat stiffly in the padded arm chair, a tight knot in the pit of his stomach.

The bishop began. "I've been waiting for you to help at the sacrament table, Troy. You are the only priest-age boy we have."

Troy squirmed in his seat. "I didn't think it was important."

"All our stewardships are. Besides, the ward needs you."

"The men do a good job," Troy told him.

"But that isn't helping you. You need to do that service."

"Why? I go to church every week."

Bishop Schmidt pulled himself taller. "Your father ordained you a priest with all its rights, privileges, and responsibilities. You even raised your right hand to sustain yourself in that meeting. You can't expect to have the blessings of the priesthood without the responsibility. You also need to set a good example for your brothers."

"That's hardly fair."

"I know, but you looked up to your dad for seventeen years, now you're the father figure in your home." Troy could feel the rising anger. "Think about it, Troy. David only had his dad for fourteen years, Alan considerably less. You were fortunate to have had him the longest."

"Fortunate!" Troy jumped up. "How can you say I was fortunate?"

Bishop Schmidt rose. "Troy, it's difficult I know, but you are nearly an adult. You're well on your way to knowing what you want to do with your life. Your brothers are still learning and need your example. Don't let them down."

Troy huffed and headed for the door even before the bishop dismissed him.

"Troy?" The bishop followed. "You aren't alone. You have your father's example, my assistance, and most of all you have our Heavenly Father's help. We don't always know why tragedy strikes, but we don't have to let it weaken us or change our eternal perspectives."

Troy turned to face the bishop. "I find it really hard not to be angry. Sometimes I can't even think straight."

"That's understandable. But think about it, okay?" Bishop Schmidt smiled warmly.

Troy could feel the tightness in his chest. His anger felt like a burning pain, as if something had taken part of his heart. "I—I'll try," was all he could say.

Troy thought about the bishop's words all through dinner and while doing the dishes. Flopping onto his bed later, Troy tried to pin down his feelings. Why does my father's death make me rebel against the truths I had always believed in? Where has my testimony gone? Troy sat up. He caught his reflection in the small oval mirror on his wall. Troy gazed at his own face. Then for a split second he could actually see his father smiling back. He tried to hold the image but when he blinked it was gone. Troy continued to stare at his now-sober face and was disappointed when the impression of his father did not return. He walked to the closet, slowly opened the door, and picked up the cap from the shelf. He held it for a moment, walked to the mirror, and placed it on his head. Troy could see his father's features on his face. As he stared at his reflection, he wondered why he looked so much like his father when he didn't have the same characteristics. Troy knew he had his father's physical features and his musical talent, but he didn't think he had his spiritual traits. Troy didn't bother wiping the tears that fell. Somehow they made him feel better.

Troy stayed unmoving until he heard the phone ring. His mind registered his mother's voice as she called down to him, but he didn't pay much attention. "Troy, can you come to the phone?" he heard her call again. "Shenade wants to talk to you."

Troy wiped his eyes. "I'm coming." He took one more look at his mirrored face, tossed the cap on the bed, and ran up the stairs. "Do you know what she wants?

"She didn't say."

"Hello."

"Hi, Troy. This is Shenade."

"Hi," he said again, twisting the coiled phone cord while he talked.

"The Young Women and Young Men's advisors are

meeting to plan the Halloween party. I think you and I need to get our ideas in before they finalize everything. I'd like to do some of those neat things you told me about."

"Okay," Troy said after a moment. He swallowed hard. "When?"

"Are you busy now? You could come over to my place. The advisors are meeting at 7:30, so we need to talk before that."

"I'll ask Mom, but I think it should be okay."

"Good. Phone me if you can't come."

"Okay, see you in a few minutes."

Troy hung up the phone and found his mother reading a Young Women's handbook in the living room. "Shenade's asked me to come over and discuss the Halloween party. Is it okay if I go now?"

Joanie nodded. "Go ahead, son." She put her book down. "You know, Troy, I'm excited about this new calling. I love working with the youth."

"It'll be fun having you work with us."

Joanie smiled. "I need you to keep an eye on your brothers while I go to the planning meeting, and I need to leave at 7:15."

"Okay, I'll be home." Troy snatched his coat from the closet and hurried out of the house.

Shenade answered the door when he rang the bell. "Come in. Let me take your coat."

Troy followed Shenade through the spacious lobby, where she hung his coat. Walking past the family room, a warm, crackling fire glowed in a grey, stone wall. The blue pile carpet made the room look regal with its white furniture. A tv played in one corner of the room and two little bodies lay on their stomachs, heads in their hands, a bowl of popcorn between them.

"Let's go in the kitchen. The family room is somewhat busy." Shenade led Troy away from the door, down the short hallway, and into the kitchen. He caught a glimpse of the livingroom on his right, the mirrored wall catching his reflection as he walked by.

Sister Johnson was stirring a steaming kettle when they entered. "Hi, Troy," she greeted. "You're just in time for some caramel popcorn. This syrup is almost done."

"Hello." Troy grinned, his hands automatically going to his pockets.

"Troy's got some neat ideas for the spook alley." Shenade grabbed a handful of popcorn just before her mother poured the cooked caramel over it.

"Good! Write them all down. The more ideas, the better."

Shenade and Troy talked and laughed for over an hour. Shenade scribbled down suggestions as rapidly as Troy could give them to her. When they finished, their paper was full of words, artwork, and figures. Sister Johnson, now sitting at the table, fingered a couple of pieces of sticky popcorn and placed them in her mouth. "I'm excited," she said. "It looks like there are lots of ideas to choose from. We'll look them all over at our meeting tonight."

Troy looked at his watch. "I gotta go. I have to babysit while Mom goes to the meeting." He started down the hall.

"I'd better hurry too." Sister Johnson left the kitchen. "Shenade! The twins need to be in bed by eight," she called back over her shoulder.

"I'd like you to come and hear some of my Halloween music. It's haunting stuff," Troy said to Shenade as he put on his coat.

"Maybe I can come over tonight if Dad gets home early."

"That'd be great if you can." He opened the door. "Thanks for the popcorn."

The wind slapped Troy in the face as he walked home. He pulled his collar up around his cheeks and hurried down the sidewalk. As he entered the house the north wind caught the door, slamming it behind him.

"Mom! I'll start the car for you if you'd like," Troy called from the bottom of the stairs.

"Thank you," his mother replied.

Troy retraced his steps out the door and sat warming the car until his mother came out.

"Shenade just called to say her dad was home and she could come over."

"Thanks," Troy said, getting out of the car.

"Thank you for warming the car. It's freezing out here."

Troy ran into the house, tossed his coat onto the floor of the closet, and picked up the phone. It seemed only minutes before he opened the door for Shenade.

Chapter Eight

Troy found it hard to be attentive in his classes the next day. His mind kept wandering back to the night before and the time he had spent with Shenade. She had curled up on the couch, knees under her chin, as he played and replayed tapes until they found the music to be used for the spook alley.

Troy watched the math teacher place equations on the board but the information never went beyond his eyes. The noon buzzer brought Troy out of his reverie, and he made his way to the lunchroom. The only familiar face he saw was Sam Livingston's. "Are you saving these seats?" he asked.

"Only for my buddies." Sam slid over to make room for Troy. Troy sat down and opened his lunch bag.

"Move over, guys!" called Kristin as she and Shenade came toward them. Kristin pushed in beside Troy, jostling the table. Troy grabbed his juice box so it wouldn't spill, but his eyes were on Shenade, who sat on the bench opposite him.

"Bob and his girls are coming, too," Shenade said.

"Well, fancy us all being at one table," said Bob, coming in with his arms wrapped around two girls. "How'd you arrange that?"

"My magnetic personality," Sam told them as he

popped a French fry into his mouth.

"It's probably Troy's refreshing personality," Carol said. Yours is old and boring."

"You've cut me to the quick!" Sam gave himself a jab to the chest. "But I don't care. Troy is my buddy."

Shenade shot Troy a quick glance but found his eyes already on her. They exchanged smiles. She looked away first. "Think we'll have this play ready for the fifth of December?" she asked no one in particular.

"You're the director," Bob said, eyeing Shenade and then Troy. "You tell us."

"I still think you should have been director. You're the person with experience," Shenade returned, pointing her finger at him.

"I only came back this year to earn a football scholarship. It's your turn to take over."

"I think the play has distinct possibilities," Sam put in joyously.

"Yeah, you would!" Pam and Carol exclaimed together.

Carol gave Sam a slap on the back. "You play the biggest idiot."

"The whole play is idiotic," stated Bob. "I'm surprised Mr. Mac is letting us do it."

"Why?" Troy questioned.

Bob explained, "Macky usually likes the serious dramatic stuff. They win more awards."

"But," Shenade interjected, "if we do a number one job on this and it takes an award, it will be a great accomplishment."

"Is that so hard to do?" Troy asked Shenade directly.

"Comedies entertain. It's the dramas that tend to win prizes." She began to tidy up her lunch wrappings as she spoke. Some of the other teens began leaving the room.

"Well, Flavius Maximus," Sam said, calling himself the character from the play, "it's time I went back to class."

"Me too." Pam hurriedly gathered her sandwich papers together. "See you last period!" she called and disappeared around the corner.

Shenade stayed behind to walk with Troy. "You're going to try out for a part, aren't you?" she asked. "There's a couple of minor roles that would be fun."

"I don't know. I'm not much for performing in front of people." Troy stopped at his locker and deposited his lunch bag inside. Grabbing his English text he turned toward his next class. "I'll think about it though."

"Good, I would like that." Shenade gave Troy a big smile as she touched his arm with her fingertips. A wave of warmth enveloped him.

"S—see you in class," Troy finally said. He could feel her eyes on him as he walked away.

"RINSE THE BLOOD OFF MY TOGA" was written in big block letters on an oversized piece of cardboard. Mr. Mac lounged casually on the stage, reading, when Troy entered. He tossed his books and jacket on the floor and made his way toward the teacher. Before he could speak, Mr. Mac asked, "Troy, could I talk to you?" His heavy bulk slid off the stage to stand in front of the teen. "Had you planned to audition for any particular role?"

"Shenade suggested that there might be a couple of minor roles I could try."

"Yes, and she's probably right, but I feel we can put your natural abilities to better use."

The room began to fill with drama students. "How so?" Troy asked.

"You have a real talent with the piano. I think I'd like you to play the background music."

Troy gulped. "But I've never played in public." He eyed the approaching students. "I can't do it."

Mr. Mac continued without heeding the protest. "You'll

have to work closely with the director to keep everything coordinated." Troy didn't have time to press the point. The buzzer sounded and a quiet hush fell across the room so Mr. Mac moved to the front of the class without looking back. Troy escaped to mingle with the group. "Today and Wednesday are auditions. Since you as a class are intent on doing this comedy, we need to complete this task no later than class time Wednesday. Some roles I've already assigned, as you know. Shenade Johnson will direct. She will choose her own assistant. Darren and Paul will do scenery and props. Alex and Trudi, lighting, and Troy will do the music."

Shenade lifted a questioning eyebrow at Troy. Troy tensed as he shook his head.

Mr. Mac continued, "Okay, the rest of you get your scripts and Shenade and I will begin listening right now."

Mr. Mac took up his spot on the stage and Shenade sat on a chair next to him. Troy felt like a sore thumb. He didn't know what to do.

"Okay, Berringer," Mr. Mac called, "The music is on the piano. Don't just stand there."

Troy shuffled across the room to the baby grand. He plopped onto the bench and began thumbing through the book. His fingers turned the pages slowly but his eyes didn't register anything. Mr. Mac hadn't heard anything he'd said. When Troy glanced over his shoulder, the teacher was already auditioning one of the students. Troy wrestled with anger and fear, but the piano was like a magnet. His fingers touched the keys. His love for the piano began to dispel some of his bad feelings. Troy ran his fingers lightly over the keys, then actually made his fingers pluck out the melody of some of the tunes. He never moved from the piano until the bell rang to end the day.

"Can I walk home with you?" Shenade asked as he shut his locker door.

"Sure," Troy answered. "Maybe it'll help me feel better."

Shenade looked questioningly at him. "What's wrong?"

"Mr. Mac didn't hear a word I said when I told him I couldn't play."

"He probably remembered your piano playing the other night and figured you could do it."

"I don't want to do it."

"Why? You're good."

"I am not good. I can't even read music very well. I play by ear."

"You were doing okay today. I listened to you."

Troy looked at her. "You did? I thought you'd be too engrossed in the auditions."

"But I heard you and it sounded all right for the first time. I think you can do it."

"But it was Dad who taught me to read music and I'm still learning."

"You can try, can't you?"

"I don't know. I've never done anything like this before. What if...?"

"Don't say what if. Just jump in with both feet like the rest of us. I've never directed before."

Troy turned away from Shenade, embarrassed at his own inadequacy. "But you're popular and the class trusts you. I could really make a mess of this."

Shenade caught up to him. "You won't. I have every confidence in you. Come on, give it a try."

Troy couldn't help liking the thought of working with Shenade. Whether he could overcome his fears and learn the music he didn't know, but he did like the idea of working with this girl.

"If you can put up with my sour notes during practices until I learn the music, I guess I can try."

"You'll do fine, just wait and see." Her smile warmed him.

They were at the Johnson gate now. "Thanks for letting

me walk home with you," Shenade said, stopping outside the gate.

"Thank you for having faith in me," Troy said, scraping his shoes on the sidewalk, his eyes on his feet. "I hope I don't let you down."

"You won't," Shenade replied as she swung open the gate and headed toward the door. "I believe in you."

After home evening on Monday Troy found time to talk to his mother. "Mom?" he asked. "I drove the truck and machinery on the farm all the time. Do you think I could take the car to school some days?"

Joanie looked at her son. "I've never even thought about it. I wonder if it's insured for you?"

"Can you find out?"

"I'll have to phone the company in Rossland, but I think I could do that."

"Tomorrow?"

"Probably, but I can't make any promises about you taking the car every day."

"I know I can't do that. But today was so cold."

"And he wants to drive his new girlfriend around," jumped in David, who had been watching television.

Troy gave him a shove with his foot, spilling a plate of crackers David was snacking on.

"Mom!" David yelled.

"You asked for that one," Joanie responded.

"Yeah!" Troy added, taking another stab at David.

Joanie placed a calming hand on Troy's outstretched leg. "Boys," she reprimanded softly. "I'll do what I can in the morning," she said to Troy, "and maybe we can work out some sort of agreement."

Troy worked after school on Tuesday but was finished early. He hurried home to eat supper with his family, then excusing himself from the table, he escaped to the piano. The music for the play was open above the keyboard. He looked at it, then at the keys, then back to the music. Slowly, painstakingly, he fingered out the melody notes with one hand. Over and over he plucked the keys until the melody sounded good. Satisfied, he began adding the base notes. He wrinkled his nose at the sound. Troy studied the music and tried again. It made little difference. The chords did not blend. It seemed the more he tried the worse it sounded. Smashing his hands down on the keyboard, he swore to himself.

"Troy's at it again," David shouted as he walked by the dining room.

"Mind your own business!" hollered Troy as he slammed the lid down on the keys. Leaning his head against the open music he tried to calm his heavy breathing. He could feel his anger turn to frustration, and tears threatened. Dad, he thought, why aren't you here to help me? Troy kept his eyes closed, his hands on the covered keyboard. Not heeding the falling tears that dripped down his cheeks, Troy let himself remember.

Mr. Berringer stood behind Troy as he tried to spread his fingers the full octave. "You're getting it, son," he said. Troy looked up into his father's smiling face and knew he was pleased. "You'll be a Mozart one of these days!"

Troy had grown considerably since then and his fingers no longer needed stretching to reach the octave, but his abililty to read music was still rusty. He wished his father were here to tutor him like he used to do."You can do it, Troy" his father encouraged. And Troy did.

Lifting his head, he wiped away the tears with the back of his hand. You can do it, he told himself and reopened the piano.

The rest of the week went quickly. Troy practised as he had never practised before. Sometimes he imagined his father next to him on the bench and it helped him deal with the frustration.

With working, practising, homework and play practice, Troy had little time to relax. His one diversion was Shenade. They talked a lot while walking home together nearly every day. At first Troy justified his time with her by telling himself he had to because of the upcoming Halloween party and the drama production. But more and more he was admitting that he just liked being with her.

The night of the Halloween party was upon them sooner than they expected. Troy spent hours at the church with the advisors and Shenade and Kristin in preparing for the evening's party. The school's drama club was also there. When Shenade had asked them to help, Mr Mac agreed the acting practice would be good experience.

"This is so neat," Kristin exclaimed as she put the last of the packaged cobwebs across the hall.

"I'm glad I'm part of the props," Shenade laughed. "I hate spiders."

"I think it's David who's going to be the hit. The makeup Mr. Mac did is unreal," Kristin said, putting the masking tape back in the box of library supplies. "I passed him coming out of the men's bathroom and I almost swallowed my gum."

The girls wound their way through the makeshift maze. The light fixtures had been darkened, some with black paper, some by removing the bulbs. They rounded the corner and passed Dracula's coffin. Troy had convinced Sam Livingston to play Dracula, so Mr. Mac was off covering Sam's face with luminous makeup. With the added touch of the black light, he would be superb.

The girls went past the last room. Shenade stopped when she heard her mother and Sister Berringer giggle. She knocked on the door, which opened immediately, but only an inch.

"Sorry," Sister Johnson informed her daughter in a

witch-like cackle. "This is out-of-bounds."

"Not to us," Shenade exclaimed.

"Something has to be a surprise for you too," Joanie Berringer spoke from behind Shenade's mother.

Shenade glanced past her mother to see two owl eyes glowing in the grey-blue lighting. She could smell the musty-damp wooden aroma of the leaves that she and her mother had collected from their backyard.

"Off you go, girlies," Sister Johnson cackled again and closed the door.

Soon everything was in place. All the props and sets were ready. Troy and Shenade, dressed as hooded monks, were to act as guides. The drama club was decked out in various costumes. Some played mad doctors, making kids handle gross innards concocted from peeled grapes; cold, cooked spaghetti; raw hamburger and liver; and bowls of steaming dry ice. The smells were as nauseating as the props.

Sam was fabulous as Dracula. He would wait until the kids were right beside him before he would sit up stiffly to drawl, "Hi, there." His hideous laugh was accompanied by two long, illuminated eye-teeth protruding from his black-ened mouth. Fake red blood drooled down his chin.

Kristin, who was dressed up as a good witch, was to arrange the kids in groups of four to take the tour through the alley. The organizers had closed off the one hallway of the church, leaving only one way in and one way out. The dance that was to follow would be held in the triple room at the end of the spook alley. All the folding doors had been opened and Mr. Mac was setting up his stereo system so the kids could dance.

Sister Shaw had organized a live game of Clue and had turned that over to Paul, who was dressed as a werewolf.

At last all was ready.

"Let's have a test run," suggested Troy.

"Who will we take through?" Shenade asked.

"I'll find some guinea pigs," Troy laughed as he headed down the hall. "Wait here."

Shortly he returned. With him, protesting vigorously, were Bishop Schmidt, Kristin's mother, the Primary president, and one of her counsellors.

"You'll never get my mom down there," Kristin said from the door.

"This will be an experience you'll always remember." Troy led the threesome down the dimly lit hall.

"That's what I'm afraid of," Bishop Schmidt said.

"I'm coming, too," Kristin called as she shut the hall door. Immediately darkness fell and the adults groaned.

Shenade played her part well. "We are entering the room of the mad scientists." Ghostly, eerie music seeped into the room from a hidden speaker. The hideous laugh of some unsuspecting victim echoed down the twisted portal. As the group fought through thick cobwebs, a flying ghost whipped past them, brushing the hair of one of the women. She screamed, but Shenade kept talking. "The mad scientist spends long, dreary hours severing the bodies of unsuspecting corpses and then tries to piece them together again. Have a glimpse at his workshop."

Dark figures loomed around the visitors. "Feel the eyeballs."

"Handle the intestines."

"Sample the brains. They're nutritious."

The bishop remained silent, but the women who were now clinging to him groaned, "Oh, gross. Oh, gross."

Somewhere in the group of adults huddled Kristin.

"Let's have Dracula get Kristin," whispered Troy to Shenade as they got closer to the coffin.

"You'll have to go single file now, people," Troy instructed. "The path is narrow."

Silence fell over the area and Shenade began to speak. "We now enter the castle of Dracula. The mad scientist disposed of him long ago so there is nothing to fear." While Shenade spoke, Troy stepped ahead and whispered to Sam.

"Come," Troy invited, "but a word of caution. Could this be the night of the full moon?"

One of the women let out a gasp and her whimper carried in the darkness. The group filed past the coffin. Sam was great. His black cape absorbed the black light, but his face stood out like a neon sign.

"Oh, that's good," remarked one of the women, trying to be brave as she passed the coffin quickly. She had no sooner spoken when Sam bolted upright and exclaimed, "Supper dearies?" Sister Ferguson, Kristin's mother, was as close as Kristin, and Sam couldn't differentiate between the two, so he spoke to them both. His luminous white hands grabbed a shoulder of each one and their screams echoed through the building. Sam let go and calmly laid back to reposition himself in the coffin.

Troy and Shenade were laughing so hard they had to stop to gain control. The only room left now was guarded by two ghastly looking figures. Shenade had not been programmed past Dracula, but her mother took over like a pro. "Welcome to the Transylvania Cemetery. This is the home of many famous celebrities. Be careful and stay together. And don't step off the path."

"I don't like this," someone said from behind.

"I'm trying to remember it's fake," Kristin said shakily.

Even Troy and Shenade were quiet. Slowly Sister Berringer opened the door. Simulated hinges creaked and their footsteps crunched on piles of dry leaves. They were in a grave yard. Crosses and headstones stood haphazardly on a little hill, some large, some small. The owl eyes that Shenade had seen earlier blinked on and off, giving the room its only light except for a pale blue glow coming from behind the largest tombstone. Once everyone was in and standing single file on the narrow path, Sister Johnson said, "Take note of the names on the tombstones. There is Jack the Ripper, Frankenstein, the Hunchback of Notre Dame, and Freddie Krugger."

"Who's Freddie Krugger?" whispered Sister Ferguson to the bishop.

"I don't think you want to know," he said.

Sister Johnson continued, "This whole graveyard will go down in history for having the most prominent citizens as residents."

Before she could say any more, a rustling sound was heard and the hillside began to quake. Long, twisted appendages curled through the top of the closest grave. The dirt and leaves and grass began to fall into a hole, slowly becoming larger.

"Oh, no!" Sister Johnson whispered frantically. "We've disturbed him. Let's get out of here!"

Sister Berringer, who had stayed by the door, cried anxiously, "Someone has locked us in!"

A ghastly rasping sound came from the grave and all eyes were transfixed on the creature that was rising from the hole in the ground.

Screams cut through the room and even Troy found himself overtaken with surges of adrenalin. Shenade was clinging to his arm, her head buried in his shoulder.

With a piercing howl, Freddie Krugger roared, "Happy Halloween!" and the lights came on. There was an instant of pregnant silence, then laughter, then chatter. Sister Berringer opened the door and everyone left.

"That was really something, wasn't it?" Shenade asked Troy as she glanced back to see their mothers replacing Freddie Krugger. "Mr. Mac did an impressive job on that makeup."

"You can say that again." Shenade and Troy went back through the spook alley to prepare for the real thing.

"No one will ever forget this," she added when they

reached the starting point. Kristin was already there. Her face was flushed, but her broad smile told Troy that all was well.

The evening was a smashing success. Modern popular songs filled the dancing area and Paul did a super job of keeping the clues coming and suspects dying in the game of Clue. Kristin, in her witch costume, stirred homemade rootbeer like a witch stirring her cauldron. The fog and foam from the dry ice billowed over the kettle.

At midnight, when closing prayer had been said, sloppy joes all eaten, and rootbeer gone, very few of the students wanted to leave.The youth leaders organized them into clean up groups and soon the area was ready for Sunday.

Shenade and Troy waited by the Johnson car for their mothers to lock up the church doors. As they waited the late night crispness clouded their breath. Troy blew a mouthful of warm air into Shenade's face. She blew back. Troy blew again and so did Shenade. A thick mist hung between them and they laughed.

"It was fun tonight, wasn't it?" Troy said breathlessly, his hands in his coat pockets.

"I'm glad we did it." Shenade blew some warm air into her hands, her eyes catching Troy's in the lamp-lit darkness.

"You cold?" he asked.

"Only my hands." She blew into her fists again.

"Here. Stick them into my coat pocket." Troy pushed his pocket open.

Shenade slipped both of her hands into the palm of Troy's hand. "Oh, you're warm," she said, her breath mist lying on his cheek.

Troy felt his heart quicken. He could not keep his eyes from the magnetic pull of her closeness. His hand tightened around her fisted hands deep in his pocket. She looked directly into the shine of Troy's eyes, then slowly followed an imaginary line down his cheek to the dimple at the corner of his mouth, and then to his lips. She glanced up to find him looking deeply at her. Troy didn't take time to think. Her closeness, her smell, her eyes captured him. Gently he touched his lips to hers. Like an electric shock his head jerked back. Shenade took a step backward pulling her hands free. Neither could release their eyes that seemed to be riveted together. They just stood looking at each other.

"You two should have waited in the car," Sister Johnson exclaimed as she came around the corner of the building to see the two teenagers standing by the car. "Come on, you'll freeze."

Shenade was the first to look away. Without a backward glance she climbed into the back seat behind her mother.

Troy's heart pounded, his face burned. He was glad it was dark as he walked slowly to the passenger side of the car. He stood looking into the darkness until his mother had taken her place in the front seat.

As soon as he had slid in beside Shenade, Troy laid his hand on top of hers. Keeping their eyes straight ahead Troy curled his fingers through Shenade's. "The winter prom's in three weeks. W—would you like to go with me?"

"I hoped you would ask." Shenade gave Troy's hand a squeeze, her smile soft and sweet.

Troy beamed. He was so happy all he could do was squeeze her hand back.

Chapter Nine

Troy hurried down to his room as soon as he reached home after church on Sunday. For the first time in months he felt like he was a winner. He could even say he was happy. As he hung up his suit he thought about last night's Halloween party. That was part of it. Everyone had had fun and the evening had ended so right. Shenade was very much a part of his life now and that pleased him.

His job was going well at the hardware. He only worked two or three days a week but it gave him spending money and let him help with expenses at home. He appreciated Brother Matthews' patience in not pushing him to drive the forklift. He'd do it someday, this he was sure, but not just right now.

Maybe it was his mother's appreciative smile, and Shenade's, as he prepared and blessed the sacrament this morning. It wasn't as hard as he thought it would be.

Troy flipped on an instrumental tape while he pulled on his jeans. Yes, he was feeling quite happy today. The closet door was open and he spotted the navy cap. He picked it up and placed it backwards on his head, the beak falling over the collar of his white shirt. As he tied his shoes he unconsciously hummed the tune filling the room. His heart felt so free and happy he couldn't help but smile at his own reflection as he passed the mirror. He pulled the cap tighter onto his head, flicked off the tape, and bounded up the stairs. He was setting the table for dinner when his mother entered, tying up her full-body apron as she walked.

"Casserole sure smells good, Mom," Troy said. "I love coming home to the smell of dinner cooking." He reached for the salt and pepper shakers from off the stove.

"It's a welcoming smell, isn't it?" Joanie watched Troy. His nearly six-foot frame moved with a lightness she hadn't seen for sometime. The cap made her take a second look. It was her husband's cap, not perched like he usually wore it coming from the field, but it was his cap. Joanie gulped. Troy looked so much like his father. A tiny knot tightened in her tummy. The cap even looked at home on her son's head. Troy had changed into dark denims but had left on his white shirt and navy print tie.

"Something wrong?" Troy noticed the intent look on his mother's face.

"N—no," she said with a little grin. "You just look happy today."

"Yeah, I do feel happy." He patted his mother's dark curls as he passed her on his way back to the dining room.

Joanie lifted the casserole from the oven. Troy was at the piano now, his fingers touching the keys lightly and briskly, the sound reflecting his mood. Joanie set the pan on the table and went back for the salad.

"Must be a girl," David announced coming from the dining room, Alan hot on his heels. "Troy's beaming today."

Troy stopped playing, spinning around on the bench to scowl at his brother.

"David!" Joanie Berringer cautioned.

"I watched Shenade follow Troy around with her eyes. And I saw him go googly-eyed at her, too."

Troy felt himself grow warm, somewhat angry with David, but also embarrassed at his inability to hide his feelings.

"You don't know anything," Troy snarled as he took a playful swipe at David's head.

"Boys. It's dinner time. Alan, please bless the food."

Alan waited. When the silence lengthened Troy looked up to see all eyes on him.

"The cap," his mother whispered aloud. Troy snapped it off, a gleam dancing in his eyes.

His mother smiled warmly. "Okay, Alan," she said.

Troy replaced the cap by the time he began playing the piano after dinner. The mood of the music was different now. Open in front of him was the drama production music. Troy practised hard, intently trying to make the pieces sound professional. It was actually coming together now. After several hours Troy retreated to his bedroom. As he lay on his bed, his tape deck running, the cap resting on his chest, Troy thought about tomorrow and wondered what kind of day it would be. It would be busy now that drama practice was every day after school or in the evenings. His hands behind his head, his eyes closed, he could see Shenade standing on the floor in front of the stage directing the players movements and lines. He could visualize the goofy antics of Samuel and Kristin as they played their characters. The practice always ended in hilarious bouts of laughter as Sam and Bob adlibbed their lines. Troy smiled to himself remembering Mr. Mac's jelly roundness bouncing with laughter as the first and second acts unfolded.

Troy picked up the cap and looked at the faded design on the front. Two different worlds, he thought. His life and future were considerably different than what he would have had with his father on the farm. Troy felt as though he was someone else living someone else's life. Yet...he sat up, turning the cap round and round as he looked at it. This life didn't seem foreign anymore. For a moment a wave of guilt swept over him and he stopped twirling the cap. How would his dad feel? Was he betraying his father by having different interests, different goals, by almost being happy away from the farm?

Troy walked to the mirror and put the cap on his head. He turned it slightly to the side, setting it the way his father wore it. Troy looked in the mirror. Immediately he was back on the farm...running in the pasture or standing in waist-high golden grain as it swayed in the western breeze. He and his dad would toss bales side by side into the second floor hay loft and always end the day sitting together at the piano.

Suddenly the happiness Troy felt earlier dissolved into a confusion of emotions. He took the cap off, placing it almost sacredly onto the closet shelf. Tears filled Troy's eyes and he wasn't sure how he felt. Where did his loyalties lie? Troy dug his fingers into his jean pockets. He had to talk to someone. He had to know what to think and do.Without hesitating, he left his room to find his mother. She was in the living room. Alan and David were lying on their stomachs playing a card game. Their mother sat on the sofa, Young Women supplies all around her. Everyone looked up when Troy entered but immediately went back to their own interests when he dropped into the arm chair. Troy leaned back, stretching his long legs out in front, his hands still buried finger deep in his pockets. He sat silently eyeing his family. When he looked at his mother, she was already watching him. Troy wanted to look away but deep down he wanted her to somehow see the distress on his face. Watching her intently, he straightened until he was sitting upright.

"Mom?" Troy blurted before his mother could speak. "How do you think Dad feels about all this?"

Alan's eyes widened and he jerked himself upright. David laid down his cards, a questioning look on his face.

"About what, Troy?" Joanie put her book down.

"This...the way we live?" He stopped momentarily. "The way we've come to live without him."

A heavy silence filled the room and everyone looked at Troy. After a long minute Troy asked again. "How do you think Dad feels when he sees us managing...and even feeling happy...without him?"

Alan's large brown eyes glared. His jaw tightened. Troy suddenly felt guilty. What a stupid thing to ask!

As if reading his thoughts Joanie turned to Troy. "Are you feeling guilty because you were happy today?"

Troy spoke rapidly. "Everything is so different now. Our goals aren't the same. We aren't doing anything Dad had planned for us."

"Troy! ....All of you. Do you remember what the purpose of life is? To learn to live happily, not just to be happy, but to learn to be happy in the situations that are presented to us."

David had moved to sit by his mother. Alan still sat stiffly on the floor. "Does that mean it's okay to be happy without Dad?" asked David.

"I know your father would want us to be happy. That's the way he was. Some things we can't change, so we have to make the best of them. Do you remember the hailstorm we had a few years ago? Alan had just had his sixth birthday. Can you remember what your father did once the storm was over?"

"He built icebergs in the water puddles," Troy said smiling. "The grain was mowed to the ground, the car roof dented and shingles from the barn had blown all over. But Dad, he just sat on the wet ground building icebergs with the hailstones in the water puddles."

"I remember that!" David laughed.

Joanie nodded. "That was how your father dealt with adversity. He couldn't change the destruction from the storm, so he found something to laugh about."

"He sure did look funny," Troy said, suddenly feeling lighter.

"I wonder how he did it?" David's voice was very

solemn. "He always smiled."

Joanie slid to the edge of the sofa, watching Alan intently, "Your father had taken out enough insurance to cover costs both for the buildings and for the crops. If you can remember, our budget was fairly tight that year, but our creditors got paid. I really believe your father had the philosophy that there are joys and blessings that come from any adversity. A person has to prepare the best he can, but the problems we have can be taken care of without them causing an emotional crisis in our lives. A lot of that, boys, comes from having a positive attitude and exercising a lot of faith."

"Didn't you ever find it difficult? You aren't like Dad," Troy said.

"No, I'm not your father but we discussed things together. We made a lot of joint decisions and I put a lot of trust in his opinions. Your dad took time to think and ponder and pray about things, so I had a lot of faith in him. His life's motto was..."

"I know," Alan interrupted, his voice sarcastic, "Grant me the serenity to accept the things I cannot change..."

"The courage to change the things I can," put in David.

"And the wisdom to know the difference," finished Troy as he shook his head at Alan, who was now standing, his fists clenched at his sides. Alan slumped down.

Joanie ignored the exchange between the two boys and added, "And your father had an overpowering trust in the Lord. So, to answer your question, Troy. Your father would be very happy to know that we were carrying on with life...not just getting by but learning to be happy in our new situation. He probably felt really bad about leaving us as he did, but he did what he could to prepare for that possibility. We have a home and car that's paid for and no farm debts. If he could have lived longer our financial situation would have been better, but we don't owe anything. That's the main thing. I know he's happy knowing we are getting on with our lives.

We'll never forget him and we'll all work hard at doing what's right so we can be with him again. So Troy, David, and Alan, be happy. Enjoy this new adventure. Look back with fond memories, but enjoy what you are doing."

Troy sat in the chair thinking about his mother's admonition. David had gone to the kitchen with their mother to find something for supper. Alan, looking very angry, had stomped off to his bedroom, slamming the door behind him. Troy thought about Shenade, school, the drama class, and his job at the hardware store. It was miraculous how everything had fallen into place. The things he was doing now had nearly clouded out the farmer life he had known just six months ago.

Troy sat with his thoughts until his mother called, "Troy, please tell Alan supper is ready."

Troy knocked on his brother's door and entered. "Supper's ready, Kiddo," he said.

"I'm not hungry," came Alan's sullen reply. He was fingering one of his model cars, the tv tray in front of him full of plastic pieces and a flattened tube of glue.

Troy sat down beside him. "That looks good," he told his brother. "Did you do it by yourself?"

"David glued in the tiny parts of the engine." Alan held the car up for Troy to see.

"So next time you'll know how and you can do it all on your own. C'mon, let's go have supper." Troy stood, hoping Alan would follow. When he didn't... "C,mon, Alan, supper's ready."

Alan looked up at Troy. "Do you think Mom's right? You know...is Dad happy that we're happy?"

Troy sat back down. "I'm sure he would want us to be happy. He always did things to make us happy so why should he be different now?"

"But I don't feel happy very often." Alan hung his head.

"Sometimes, I don't either, and I feel guilty when I do feel happy. That's why I asked Mom about it." Troy pushed a loose blonde curl from Alan's forhead. The little boy looked up.

"I don't feel guilty, I feel mad," Alan's teeth clenched.

"Sometimes I get mad, too."

"You do?" Alan straightened.

"Sure." Troy gave his little brother a reassuring smile.

"Why do you get mad?"

Troy pulled Alan toward him. "Probably for the same reason you do. I feel happy and figure I don't have the right to be...or something is bothering me and Dad isn't here to talk to."

Alan laid his head on Troy's shoulder. "Then Mom's probably right, eh? Dad would want us to be happy."

"I think so. I like being happy. I wouldn't want to be miserable and sad all the time."

"I'm trying not to be either. But I'm tired of doing pushups."

Troy smiled, giving Alan's biceps a squeeze. "But it's sure giving you muscles. You'll soon be as big as me."

Suddenly Troy had an idea. "Hey, come with me, Alan. I have something for you." He jumped from the bed, pulling Alan behind him. They scurried down the stairs, jumping the last step, and hurried into Troy's room. Troy left Alan in the doorway and went straight to the closet. The navy blue cap sat where he had left it. He lifted it down, looked at it, and then at Alan.

"Here, you have this, and every time you feel sad or angry put it on." Troy placed the cap on Alan's head. It slid down over his ears, covering his almost-blonde eyebrows.

Both boys giggled. Alan took the cap off, holding it tightly by the back seam. "I can have this? You wouldn't let anyone touch it before."

Troy gulped down the tightness that was filling his throat. He took the cap from Alan and shortened the adjustment strap at the back. "I want you to have it." He placed the cap back on Alan's head. "When I felt sad, I wore it straight. When I felt happy, I twisted it backwards." He flipped the cap around so the beak was over Alan's shirt collar. "And when I felt goofy, I wore the beak over one ear." He pulled the cap halfway back so it lay over Alan's ear.

Alan laughed. "Dad did that sometimes."

"Yeah, he did. Now...so can you." Troy stood back, looking his little brother up and down.

Alan turned the cap so that it sat on his head the right way. He looked into Troy's mirror for a minute, then said, "Thanks, Troy."

Troy put his arm around Alan. "No problem. Now, let's go eat before Mom and David eat it all." Alan shifted the cap again, glanced one more time into the mirror, then led Troy from the room.

Neither Joanie nor David commented when the two boys came to the table. David did, however, wait for Alan to remove the cap before beginning the blessing on the food. Alan smiled at Troy as he clutched the cap in his hand.

The north wind bit into Troy's face as he hurried to work after school on Wednesday. Mr. Matthews had called him that morning, asking him to come in to help unload an extra big shipment. When Troy arrived, Tom Porter and some of the other employees were standing at the back door, their conversation buzzing like bees.

"Hey!" Troy called hurrying over. "What's up?"

Before anyone could answer, the group separated to allow their boss and Les Thoms, the yard supervisor, through. "Oh good, you're here, Troy. I have to get Les to the hospital. You will have to unload the truck." Mr. Matthews didn't stop walking. He was nearly pulling Les Thoms by the hand. Troy glimpsed down to see Les' hand wrapped in a large towel, already a bright red.

Without thinking he said, "Sure thing."

The employees slowly returned to their work. "What happened?" Troy asked Tom as he put on his heavier coat to go outside.

"I'm not sure, but I think some of the metal strapping snapped in the cold, slashing Les' hand. It sure bled lots." He zipped up his coat. "Let's get that truck unloaded."

Troy stopped short. The fork lift! Mr. Matthews expected him to drive the fork lift! Suddenly his knees went weak.

Tom was outside huddling against the wind. "You unload the plywood first. I'll help line it up on the piles then tag it while you unload the other pallets." He turned to see Troy still anchored in one spot. "Come on before I freeze to death!" Troy consciously moved his heavy feet toward the tractor. Tom had his gloves on waiting. "Do you want me to drive again and you tag?"

Troy just about said yes, but somewhere in the back of his mind a voice, much like his father's, said, "You can do it."

Troy looked at the fork lift then back at Tom. "N–No," he found himself saying. "I'm going to do it today."

"Sure thing." Tom began straightening sheets of plywood on the existing pile.

Troy stepped onto the tractor. The shock of the cold seat made him jump. He glanced around, noticed he was alone, and touched the key. His heart beat hard against his chest. His temple thumped. Troy jerked his hand away. It's time, a feeling more than a thought told him. You can do it.

Troy gave the key a sharp twist. The engine roared and the tractor gave a jerk. Troy grabbed the steering wheel with both hands. He held tight for a moment.

"Take the little pile off first!" Tom called. "It's the 3/4 inch stuff."

Troy swallowed the lump he was choking on. Licking his lips he pulled the gearshift to put the tractor in reverse. His hands tightened on the wheel. Like the Little Engine that

Could, Troy found himself saying aloud, "I can do it. I can do it."

He backed away from the parking stall and drove to the side of the 18-wheeler flat deck. The 3/4 inch plywood was on the back of the trailer. Troy grabbed the black knob and pushed it forward. The fork lifted. Just as though he was working on the farm, the old skill returned and some of the fear subsided. Troy advanced slowly, adjusting the height of the forks as he approached the stack of plywood. He carefully slid the forks under the pile. Tilting the front so the plywood would slide further back onto the forks, Troy gulped in a mouthful of air. He had not realized he was holding his breath.

Troy put the tractor in reverse. Slowly he began releasing the clutch. His breath was coming in short pants and he felt as though he were running a race. He glanced up to see where Tom was. In that instant his boot slipped off the clutch and the tractor lurched. Troy grasped the steering wheel. In a flash his whole life passed before his eyes. "Oh!" he hollered, slamming on the brake. Again the tractor lurched; the plywood bounced but stayed in place.

Troy took a second to catch his breath. He looked around for Tom, hoping he had not seen the mishap. Tom wasn't in sight.

"Whew," sighed Troy. He pressed his foot solidly to the clutch and gave the tractor a little gas. Without further incident, except for the persistent butterflies in his stomach, Troy and Tom stacked the wood before the store closed at six. Robert Matthews never did return that evening.

Tom didn't say anything to Troy when they finished, but as they left the yard Tom gave Troy a slap on the back. Troy felt he was part of the regular staff now, not just a part-time joe-boy doing odd jobs. He had a purpose.

No one made an issue about Troy's driving the fork lift. It was as though he had always been doing it. Les Thoms had a nasty cut on his arm and thumb and had to work indoors while it was so cold. Tom and Troy took over the outside jobs.

Chapter Ten

The weather was clear but cold the night of the Winter Prom. Snow blanketed all the lawns and a thin layer covered the roads. Troy left home to pick up Shenade at 8:30, dressed in his best pants and his new matching sweater. The shirt and tie had belonged to his father, but he didn't seem to mind. The whole outfit looked new.

He parked the car in front of Shenade's house and went to her door. "Fancy you answering the door," Troy joked, as Dr. Johnson let him in. "I don't get that privilege very often."

"There's a first time for everything. Come on in."

"Is Shenade ready?"

"She's been ready for hours."

"Daddy!" Shenade protested from behind her father.

Troy looked past the doctor to see Shenade in a peach-colored, knee length dress. Her green eyes stood out under a light touch of makeup. "Hi, Shenade." She could see the look of approval in his eyes. "Are you ready to go?"

"Please drive carefully," Sister Johnson said, stepping into the hallway. "The streets are slippery tonight."

"The school's not far, so we'll be fine," Shenade reassured her.

"Will you be home by 12:30?" asked Dr. Johnson.

"As close as we can," said Troy as he helped Shenade with her coat.

"Have a good time."

"We will!" the teenagers called as they closed the door.

As soon as Troy stepped out of the car in the school parking lot he could hear the music pounding out its aggressive beat. He hurried to open the passenger door for Shenade. "I think I'll leave my coat in the car," Shenade said as she got out. "I don't want to have to search through three hundred others when we leave."

Troy shut and locked the door. He slid his hands into his pockets. "If the number of cars is any indication of the number of kids at the dance, it doesn't look like there's twenty coats to search through."

"Oh, you can't judge by that," Shenade replied, "It's early yet. And lots of kids don't bring their cars to these dances.

"Why?" Troy stopped short of the open main doors of the school and watched a brilliantly colored van race noisily into the parking lot.

"That's the reason." Shenade stepped into the warm foyer. "They're probably drunk." Troy watched the van screech to a halt.

"That wonderful specimen of so-called He-Man is one of the school's worst problems. He's been arrested several times for possession of drugs and alcohol." The two youths walked down the large illuminated hallway toward the gym. "He's totalled two vehicles already this year and is probably driving without a license."

Troy glanced quickly behind him as a group of boisterous kids entered the school. "I've seen him around but he isn't in any of my senior classes. He sure looks old enough."

"Oh, he is. Brad's nearly twenty and takes a few junior courses. I think he goes to school to keep the drugs going."

Troy paid their admissions and they entered the gym.

The Winter Wonderland decorations removed all signs of sports from the hall. "Somebody did a super job." Troy spun a complete turn to view the whole room.

"Hi, kids," a voice greeted.

"Hello," Shenade and Troy replied simultaneously, as Mr. Prowley, the principal, went by. They watched him go towards the group of clamorous youths standing at the admissions table, but they couldn't hear any of the conversation that followed.

"Hi, guys," called Sam Livingston as he jumped from the stage.

"Are you the one picking our music for the evening?" Shenade asked once Sam had reached them.

"Someone has to. I mean Macky's pretty good, but my taste in dance music is more modern, don't you think?"

"I suppose, if you like chicken dancing," Shenade laughed. "This character felt the dance in the spring was too dull so he decided to liven it up."

"And I did, didn't I?" Sam beamed.

"You sure did and almost got yourself arrested."

"But that wasn't my fault," Sam's chin dropped, a pout on his lips.

"What happened?" asked Troy when the three were sitting at a table.

"We always get a few kids at our dances who mess things up because of liquor," Shenade said more seriously. "Sam was just being his normal self and security wanted him to leave."

"Disgusting, eh? And all I was doing was being myself." He slumped resignedly back into his chair.

"But being yourself is not always what's acceptable, you clown," put in Kristin, who had heard Sam's last comment as she approached the table. He sat up and slid out a chair for his fellow drama friend to sit on.

"But I like being me," he pouted again.

"Then you'll have to take the abuse," Kristin retorted, ruffling Sam's tightly reddish curls.

Troy and Shenade exchanged grins then turned their attention to the increasing activity in the room. The table they were at filled quickly with drama students and the chatter was lively and spirited. Bob and Carol were the last of their group to arrive. Carol appeared to be angry but Troy noticed her silence even more. Bob grabbed Kristin and swung her out onto the dance floor. Sam took this as a cue and asked Carol to dance. At first Troy thought she'd refuse, but instead she shrugged her shoulders and accepted Sam's offer. Troy looked at Shenade and then at the crowd. The second time he glanced at her she was looking at him. "D—do you want to dance?" he asked, his eyes not meeting hers.

"I'd like to. If you want to."

Troy slid his chair from the table and held his hand out for Shenade. She allowed him to lead her onto the dance floor. They began to mingle with the fast moving crowd. Quite easily Troy found himself relaxing, even finding the courage to try some of the jive steps he'd learned at dance practice in Rossland.

When they returned to the table a very agitated Sam sat alone. "Hey, you guys," he said excitedly. "We have a problem."

"What's wrong?" Shenade asked. "And where's Carol?" She looked around for the other girl.

"She went with Kristin."

"Where?" Troy could hear the concern in Shenade's voice.

"To the ladies' room, I think."

"So, what's up?" asked Troy.

"It's Bob," Sam said almost angrily. "That turkey's been drinking. Carol is upset."

"I'm surprised she got in the car with him," said Shenade. "He knows she doesn't allow him to drink and drive with her."

"I guess he was late getting to her place so he just honked and she got in."

"So where is he?" asked Troy.

"He went for some cider and doughnuts," Sam motioned to the refreshment table.

"Where's everyone else?" Shenade surveyed the crowd.

"Out there somewhere." Sam's sweep of his arm took in the whole room.

"Here he comes." Troy squirmed uneasily in his seat. Bob's voice could be heard even before they saw him.

"And the girls are with him," Shenade added.

Sam stood and waited for the trio.

"D—do—don't make such a big deal about it—" Bob slurred."I've only had a couple beers— And besides, I'll have some of these doughnuts and hot cider, then I'll be okay." He clumsily sat the tray on the table, slopping cider on the paper plate full of doughnuts. "Here, I brought enough for everyone."

Carol looked disgusted. She moved around to sit by Sam, ignoring Bob's offer.

I think Mr. Prowley's getting upset with Bob," Shenade said to Troy during one of the waltzes.

"It looks like he's getting more and more drunk." Troy turned in so he could see Bob. "Carol hasn't danced with him all night."

"I know," said Shenade, her voice sad. "Why do some people have to drink to have fun? Look at the Halloween party. No one was drinking there."

"I don't know," was all Troy could say.

Without warning the music stopped. Troy and Shenade stood with the other dancers as Mr. Prowley and two security guards escorted a group of kids from the gym. Then the music began again and the dance resumed.

"Well, at least they'll get home safe," Kristin said when

Troy and Shenade sat down.

"Why's that?" asked Troy.

"This dance is a 'Safe-Prom' night like the 'Safe-Grad' program. If the kids have been drinking the security guards escort them to taxis and collect their car keys. The kids can pick them up on Monday at school or a parent can pick up the vehicle anytime."

"Yeah," Sam exclaimed, "every year some kid gets hurt or killed because of booze."

From across the room Bob was staggering toward them. Carol hurried ahead of him. "Can someone help this guy? He's getting disgusting," she said.

Bob stumbled to the table and collapsed on a chair. Immediately his head flopped forward and his breathing grew heavy.

"Oh, swell," Carol grumbled. "Now he's passed out. I'm going home," she said stepping away.

"You can't walk," Shenade told her. "It's too cold, and you're not dressed to walk."

"What am I supposed to do? My parents aren't home and he isn't in any shape to drive." She motioned to Bob.

"They won't give him his car keys anyway," Sam informed them.

"I know," sighed Carol.

"I'll take you home," Troy volunteered. "And Bob, too."

"He can pick up his car on Monday. It'll probably do him good to ride the bus in." Sam slid back his chair as he spoke.

Shenade looked at Troy. "Carol lives close to the city centre, but Bob lives about eight miles out of town on the road to Cedarside. Your Mom may not let you take her car out on the gravel road."

"I'm a farm boy, remember. We'll run Carol home, then I'll stop off to change my clothes and get Mom's permission. I think she'll be okay with it." He pushed away from the table.

"Here, I'll help get Bob in the car," Sam told Troy. He lifted Bob with Carol's help and started across the dance floor toward the exit.

"I'll come with you," Shenade spoke to Troy as they followed the others. "I'll keep you company on the way home."

"I'd appreciate that, but I think you'd better get permission too." Troy held the door open for the group and Sam coaxed Bob out into the fresh air. He mumbled and squirmed but Carol and Sam kept tight their hold.

"I'd like to put jeans on, too," Shenade said. "I'll do it quickly while you're changing."

Troy unlocked his car doors and he and Sam crammed the sleeping hulk into the back seat. Shenade let herself into the passenger side while Troy started the car. Carol had slid in beside Bob and let his head rest on her shoulder.

"I'll go find Kristin now," Sam hollered. "You guys take it easy." He waved as he ran into the warm building.

"Thanks loads," Carol said when they reached her home. She climbed from the car. "I appreciate what you're doing for Bob. He really is all right. Alcohol just makes him act like a jerk."

"I know," Shenade smiled reassuringly. "We'll get him home."

"Thanks again for the ride." Carol spun on her heels and ran for the house.

Troy hurried home. He stopped long enough to let Shenade off at her place, then leaving the car running outside his yard, sped into the house.

Joanie heard the door slam and went to meet her son. Troy was already unbuttoning his shirt as he explained Bob's situation to his mother. Joanie shook her head but gave Troy her consent to use the car to take Bob home.

"I'm taking Shenade with me," Troy said. "She's changing into warm clothes as well."

"I'm glad. I would worry with you alone on a strange road."

"I've been on it a couple times delivering lumber, so it's not totally unknown." Troy darted downstairs and was back up just as quick. "I'll be back as soon as I can," he called to his mother as he zipped up his coat.

"Drive carefully," she called back.

"Sure thing," was all she heard.

Troy turned the car around and honked the horn outside the Johnson home. Immediately the door opened and Shenade ran out.

"I see our baby is sleeping soundly." Shenade glanced back at the youth sprawled on the rear seat.

"He hasn't moved." Troy signalled and turned onto the main highway. "Do you know where this guy lives?" he asked.

"Yes, but I thought you did too."

"I know approximately, but I don't think I'd recognize the farm in the dark."

"We'll find it together then."

"We do lots of things better together, don't we?" said Troy. He was thinking of the drama production as he spoke. He caught a glimpse of Shenade's smile under the glow of the light standards lining the road. Troy drove quietly along the highway and turned at the junction leading to Cedarside. The hard surface on the road ended about half a mile from the highway.

Troy slowed his speed down to compensate for the thick gravel. Heavy traffic had grooved the surface causing the low car to grate over the higher mounds of rock, making it sound as though hundreds of tin cans were dragging under the car.

"It needs grading again," Troy told Shenade. "I hate it when the gravel rubs the undercarriage."

"It's more noisy than harmful, isn't it?"

"I think so," Troy said, carefully maneuvering a speed corner.

The glow of headlights from an oncoming car popped up just as Troy started up a hill. He slowed to a crawl and pulled right over to the edge of the road. The oncoming car seemed to do the same. A spray of gravel caught the side of the small car, but none hit the windshield.

"You know something, Troy?" Shenade questioned, looking at the silhouette of the driver. "You're different from other guys."

Troy glanced at her quickly. "How do you figure that? I have two arms, two eyes, and a new crop of zits every week."

Shenade laughed. "Yeah, you have those all right, but you're still different." She hesitated. "I think it's because you're not predictable."

"Is that good or bad?"

"Oh, it's not something that needs to be categorized good or bad. It's just an observation."

"Oh," Troy submitted. Bob snorted and groaned from behind. "Is he waking up?" Troy asked.

Shenade looked in the back seat. "No, he's just restless."

"How much farther?" Troy asked again.

"How many speed corners have we taken?"

"Just one."

"Then we'll have to take one more to our left and Bob lives on the corner of the second intersection from there."

"This speed corner?" Troy asked slowing at the turn.

"Yes. Green's have a large yard light over their house and one near the corrals so we should be able to find it easily."

Troy and Shenade remained silent as they surveyed the surrounding darkness. Shortly they arrived at the second crossroads and Shenade pointed while explaining. "You can go in the first driveway. It circles the farm house so you can go right around."

Troy flicked on the signal light, glanced in his rearview mirror, and negotiated the turn. He parked close to Green's back stairs and let Shenade run up to knock on the door. Troy went immediately to Bob, pulled him to a sitting position, then struggled to get his limp body off the back seat. Half dragging Bob, he started up the stairs.

"Let me help," said a full male voice from above as Troy felt Bob's weight lighten.

"We appreciate you bringing our boy home," Mrs. Green spoke as she held open the door for her husband and Troy. "I hate it when he drinks."

"Someday this boy'll get himself killed," said Mr. Green, who had dropped his son on the sofa. "Maybe then he'll learn."

Shenade and Troy looked at each other, then made for the door. "Thanks again, kids," Mrs. Green said. "We do appreciate this."

"Our pleasure," Troy told her. They waved good-bye as they left.

The two youths got into the car and started out of the yard. They waited for a car to pass before proceeding onto the Cedarside road back to Inglewood. The lights from the city filled the sky with a dull orange glow.

"I appreciate you coming with me," Troy spoke somewhat timidly, his hand reaching out to touch Shenade's.

"I'm glad I came, too. I enjoy doing things with you." Shenade curled her fingers around Troy's.

"Even when I get kind of nerdy?" he asked, butterflies bouncing in his stomach.

"Even when you get kind of nerdy." Shenade gave Troy's hand a squeeze.

Oncoming headlights appeared up ahead. Troy glanced quickly in his rearview mirror and saw lights in the distance behind him. He released Shenade's hand so he could use both of his to control the car on the gravel. "Sorry," he said simply.

"It's okay. It's safer."

Troy drove quietly for a few minutes then asked, "Can

you believe we're going to be graduating in six months?"

"Unless I flunk," Shenade teased.

"Never!" Troy laughed. "If anyone flunks, it'll be me."

"Are you concerned about your grades?" She turned slightly to look at him.

"No, I'm more concerned about graduation."

"Why?"

"Because I'd like you to be my escort for grad. I mean, my date. I—I—I didn't want to graduate in Inglewood until lately." He hurried on. "But I'd like to go with you."

Shenade was chuckling to herself. "If you'd stop rattling on, I'd tell you that I'd like to go with you. It would look funny if we didn't go together."

Troy, slowing down the car, looked briefly at Shenade and then back to the road. The approaching headlights were closing in so Troy pulled the car tighter to the edge of the road.

"You do realize," Shenade was saying, "the kids in the drama class consider you and I a couple."

"I know. The guys tease me quite often but.." He stopped speaking to concentrate on his driving. The first speed corner was coming up. Dimming his lights for the oncoming car he entered the wide turn.

"Are you all right with that?" Shenade asked as Troy gave the car a touch more gas to make the corner.

Troy did not have time to answer. As he angled the car to complete the corner, the oncoming vehicle was close enough for Troy to see the courtesy lights above the windshield. "Boy! Is he moving!" Troy exclaimed, holding tighter to the steering wheel.

"And all over the road!" Shenade cried.

Troy pulled harder to the right and felt the rear wheels grab the loose gravel on the road's edge. The approaching vehicle was almost on them when the small car began to fishtail as if it were on ice. Troy tried to ride with the motion so as not to roll the car, but the oncoming truck was now taking the speed corner in the wrong lane. Last second efforts to gain control proved fruitless and Troy aimed the car the best he could for the ditch. "Hang on! We're going in!"

Fear gripped him as the car bumped off the road and into the ditch. His headlights caught a road approach in front of him. Shenade remained stiff and silent. The downward momentum made the car accelerate and Troy fought to keep the car upright on the ditch bank. They hit the road approach square on. Instead of stopping, the angle of the approach acted as a catapult and the lightweight vehicle flew into the air. Troy heard Shenade gasp.

"Shenade!" he cried as he reached out to grab her.

Chapter Eleven

The next instant the car hit the ground solidly. Glass, metal, and plastic shattered and flew all around them. All was black, but Troy was aware of the slowing onward movement of the car. A sharp grating sound was the last thing that registered.

When Troy opened his eyes the air around him was thick and cloudy. His first thought was for his passenger.

"Shenade!" he cried as he spat broken teeth and blood through cracked and split lips. Her motionless body lay crumpled against the passenger door. "Shenade!" he called again. Neither his voice nor his touch brought a response.

Troy wrenched on the door beside him. Finally it popped open, but it took all his strength to push it wide enough to get out. His knees wobbled, his head spun, and nausea swept over him. As he vomited, his face and chest were racked with pain and he feared he'd pass out again. Steadying himself on the car, he straightened the best he could, wiped his face on the sleeve of his jacket, and staggered to the passenger door. He pulled on the handle. It wouldn't budge. He slid his hand through the broken glass to check the door lock. Tears ran down his face, fear tore at his heart. "Don't be dead!" he cried hysterically. Again and again he pulled on the door. Amidst his sobs, Troy could hear voices from far away. Ignoring them, he stumbled back to the driver's door.

The dust and smoke registered now, and a new fear filled his mind. "Fire!" he exclaimed. He had to get Shenade out. As carefully as he could, Troy dragged the girl over the gear console and the driver's seat and out onto the grass. He picked her up, ignoring the searing pain in his back and chest. Staggering away from the wreck, he felt for a level spot with his foot and lowered Shenade onto the cold earth. Removing his jacket, he covered her.

"Hey!" a voice hollered. "Are you all right?"

The voice closed in on Troy and a beam of light shone in his face. Troy was crying steadily now. "Please don't let her die! Please don't let her die!" He turned back to Shenade and knelt beside her. He stroked her forehead gently and closed his eyes. "Please, God, don't let her die." Shenade stirred briefly, then remained still.

The man who had spoken hesitated only a second when his light caught sight of the boy's face. Running back to his tanker truck, he grabbed a roll of paper towels and hurried back to the kids. Stuffing a wad of towelling into the boy's hand, he was surprised to see Troy snatch it up and tuck it under Shenade's head instead of mopping up some of the blood from his face.

The trucker shook his head but said nothing. He watched the boy kneeling beside the girl, his hands caressing her face and hair. The sound of a siren turned the trucker's attention back to the Cedarside Road. He hurried to meet the police and the Inglewood ambulance he had radioed for.

It was only minutes before Troy was laid on a stretcher, a moist dressing over his mouth. Shenade lay on the stretcher opposite, secured to a spinal board. Troy kept his eyes on her for any signs of movement. His body shook, his head and back throbbed.

"She's breathing on her own and I don't feel anything broken," the paramedic reported, "but she is unconscious."

The flashing red lights illuminated the country road ahead. As soon as they reached the city limits, Troy suddenly thought of the car and what his mother would think. Shaking his head, he closed his eyes. "Oh no!" he cried softly.

Joanie Berringer fidgeted with the dial on the television. She glanced at her watch. 1:30. I wish those kids would get home, she thought to herself. Joanie made it a habit to either stay up until all her kids were home or leave a note to have them wake her. She had been to bed once, but Dr. Johnson had phoned at 1:00 to check on the kids, so Joanie decided to stay up. She felt agitated but knew Troy would be careful. He'll walk in anytime, she told herself. He's just got sidetracked talking with Shenade. She liked Shenade and knew that she had made it easier for Troy to adjust to his new life.

Joanie jumped when her doorbell rang. "Can I take anymore?" the thought escaped her lips. She slowly opened the door. Her knees weakened and panic swept through her when the open door revealed a uniformed policeman.

"Mrs. Berringer?" he asked. "Your son is at Call County Memorial Hospital. He's been in an accident."

Joanie felt her body weaken but managed to steady herself. "How bad is he—? Is he dead?" Tears filled her eyes, but she gulped down the urge to cry.

"I don't know," the officer told her. "Come and I'll drive you down."

Joanie went for her coat and started for the door. Remembering David and Alan, she ran up the stairs to their room. "David," she whispered aloud. "David!" Her second son opened his eyes. "David, Troy's been in an accident. I'm on my way to the hospital."

David's sleepy eyes widened and he swung himself out

of bed. "Troy? Is he hurt bad?"

"I don't know. The police are here to take me to him. Take care of your brother. I'll be home as soon as I can."

"Phone me, okay? I'll lie on the sofa so I can stay awake." Joanie nodded and left with the policeman.

They arrived at the hospital emergency entrance just as Dr. and Mrs. Johnson pulled up in their car. "Joanie!" Betty Jean Johnson cried. The two women embraced each other and Dr. Johnson held the door open for them. He led them to the emergency cubicles and to their teenagers.

Nurses were with both kids taking pulses and blood pressures. Joanie saw Shenade first lying very still. Her face was unmarked and free of visible injury. Dr. Johnson hurriedly spoke to the orderly, but Joanie went into the next cubicle to find her son semi-seated on a bed.

"I'm sorry, Mom," were the first words Troy spoke. "I'm so sorry."

Joanie's relief at seeing her son alive was so great that she put her arms around his neck and cried. "I'm sorry," Troy said again. "I crashed your car."

Joanie straightened. Fresh tears ran freely down both their faces. Troy's face was bruised, raw and bleeding. His lips were bloody and cracked and swollen, and Joanie could see that some of his teeth were missing or broken.

"Don't worry about the car, son, as long as you are okay."

Troy grasped his mother's hand. His voice shook as he spoke. "M—M—Mom, if Shenade dies, I'll kill myself."

"Troy!" his mother gasped.

"I mean it, Mom. It's my fault she's hurt."

"Not according to the police," Dr. Johnson's voice interrupted.

"Dr. Johnson?" Troy's words were slurred. "How is she?"

"Shenade is slipping in and out of consciousness. Her

injuries aren't as visible as yours. She has a nasty lump on the side of her head and a small laceration on her ankle."

"Is she going to be okay?"

"I think so. We won't know the full extent of her injuries until we do some x-rays and until she is fully conscious. What about you?"

"I guess I'm going down for X rays, too, as soon as they finish with Shenade. At least that's what they told me."

"So just relax. I've sent for Brother Matthews. He's coming down and we'll administer to both of you."

Troy leaned back against the pillow. "Have a rest now," Joanie said, brushing a tuft of hair off his forehead. "I'll look in on Shenade."

Troy nodded and closed his eyes.

Joanie found Betty Jean wiping Shenade's lips with a damp cloth. Shenade stirred and opened her eyes. "Mom?"

Betty Jean smiled. "I'm here," she answered, but Shenade was already sleeping again.

"So, do we know what happened?" Joanie asked after flipping the opening of the cubicle to glance at her restless son.

Dr. Johnson lifted his daughter's eyelids. "The police said that a half-ton truck forced these kids off the road. There was an oil tanker following them and the driver said Troy acted like a pro keeping the car upright once it hit the ditch. From what he saw, Troy avoided a head-on collision."

After phoning David to reassure him, Joanie spent her time going back and forth between cubicles. Troy received stitches to close the wounds in his mouth and on his face. Shenade required four stitches on her ankle. The X rays revealed no broken bones, but Shenade would be hospitalized with a concussion, and Troy could be sent home, as his injuries were torn muscles and ligaments in his back. He was told that the twisted position he was sitting in while trying to hold Shenade when the car hit the ground had caused the muscles along his spine to be torn away. The steering wheel and dash had caused the damage to his face and teeth.Brother Matthews came and helped administer, first to Shenade, and then to Troy. After a few words of consolation, he left.

Troy eased himself off the bed and painfully went to see Shenade. Tears sprang instantly to his eyes when he looked at her lying silent and still, flat on her back without a pillow.

"Shenade," Troy whispered.

She opened her eyes when he clasped her hand in his. A slight knowing smile crossed her lips, and she closed her eyes again. "Please forgive me," he cried softly and laid his swollen lips against her warm, smooth forehead. "I'll be back early in the morning," he told her. He hoped she could hear him.

Dr. Johnson placed his arm around the boy. "Don't blame yourself. You did the best you could. Come on," he said to Joanie, "let me take you home. Betty Jean is going to stay here tonight so she can be here when Shenade is fully conscious."

Troy stopped. "I'm staying too," he said matter-of-factly.

"You need a good sleep, Troy." The doctor led him to a wheelchair in the corner. "Home is the best place for you."

Troy was suddenly too tired to protest. He allowed himself to be pushed to the car in the wheelchair. As Dr. Johnson drove, Troy's mind reeled to and fro. Several times on the way home he would drift off into a fitful sleep, only to be awakened by haunting images of the accident. When he opened his eyes, any oncoming headlights diffused into myriads of dancing sparklers on a pitch-black backdrop, causing nausea to sweep over him.

Dr. Johnson helped Joanie get Troy into the house and onto her bed. "I want him upstairs for a day or two," she insisted. "I want to be able to keep an eye on him."

David, who was still awake when his mother got home,

scurried down to Troy's room for his pajamas. He struggled, with his mother's help, to get Troy undressed and settled into bed. After accepting a glass of water to swallow some pain killers, Troy slid under the covers. Joanie sat on the chair at the foot of the bed so she could watch over her oldest son.

Dr. Johnson took David to the door and briefly explained the accident to him. "Phone me," he told David, "if you think I am needed."

"Sure thing," David replied.

"Go to bed, son," Joanie suggested to David when he returned to his mother's bedroom. "It's nearly three o'clock."

"Where are you going to sleep?" he asked.

"I'm going to sit here for awhile, then I'll lie down on the sofa," she replied.

"You sleep in my bed," David invited. "I'll sleep on the sofa."

Joanie arose from her chair and led David back to his room. "No," she whispered. "I don't want to wake Alan up, and I have a feeling Troy will be awake on and off until morning."

"Okay, but call me if you need something."

"Thank you, and I appreciate you waiting up. Good night, son," she said as she gave him a hug.

"Good night, Mom."

Troy was sitting on the edge of the bed when his mother returned. "I can't sleep." Troy's voice was almost angry. "I keep seeing the car flying through the air and the ground coming up at me." His voice shook and his body trembled. "All I can think of is how I hurt Shenade. And Mom—" he exclaimed, "I ruined your car!"

Troy winced as Joanie sat next to him, pain spasms shooting through his back. "Don't worry about all that now. You are safe and Shenade is going to be fine."

"I don't know," Troy cried anxiously. "They said she's got a concussion. I know she'll never speak to me again."

"Troy."

"She won't, Mom!"

"If she had been driving when that truck forced you off the road, would you turn away from her, or refuse to speak to her?"

"No!"

"Then give her the same credit, too, okay?"

Troy sat silent, his mind struggling through a collage of images and thoughts. "And the car—?"

"We'll take care of that in the morning. The police had it towed into town, and we do have insurance, so we'll have to make do until we sort it all out."

Troy looked at his Mom. "I love you."

"I love you, too, Troy. I'm thankful the Lord was watching over you." Troy turned painfully to receive the hug his mother gave him. "Metal and glass can be replaced," she said, "but lives can't. Now lie down and try to sleep. The medication should soon help you to relax."

"Thanks, Mom."

"You're welcome, son." With that, Joanie again took up her vigil from the chair.

Chapter Twelve

"Shenade, don't die!" Troy screamed, his head tossing from side to side.

Joanie sprang from her chair. "Troy! What's the matter?"

"I can't turn it off. I can't get rid of those images!" he cried shakily as he agonizingly pulled himself upright.

Joanie helped him sit. Tears filled her eyes. "I wish I could take it away, Troy. But I can't."

Troy looked forlornly at his mother. "What can I do?'

"There's nothing you can do but wait. It takes time for memories to fade. Try to sleep now, okay?"

Troy nodded as he closed his eyes. Speaking softly he said, "I know Dr. Johnson gave me a blessing in the hospital but I feel like saying my prayers."

Joanie knelt by the bed. "A good idea. You close your eyes and stay there. I'll pray for both of us." Joanie bowed her head.

Troy was breathing more calmly when Joanie finished. She stayed on her knees, looking at her son. "Thank you Heavenly Father," she said quietly and lowered her head in gratitude.

Troy had Dr. Johnson take him to the hospital early the next morning. Joanie protested his going but knew Troy would not relax until he had talked to Shenade.

"Betty Jean can go home to the twins if you're there to sit with Shenade," Dr. Johnson told Troy.

"Do you know how she is?" Troy asked.

"Shenade regained consciousness about four this morning. She has some aches and pains but she'll be fine. Right now our main concern is her memory." Troy looked hard at the doctor. "When Mrs. Johnson called me at six this morning, she said that Shenade knew who she was and that she remembered all of us, but details surrounding the accident are gone. She doesn't remember how she came to be in the hospital."

"Is that serious?" Troy asked, a spasm of pain causing him to wince.

"I don't think so. It should be only temporary. We'll know more soon."

They arrived at the hospital and Troy slowly followed Dr. Johnson into one of the wards. His feet were heavy, and with each step he groaned. Dr. Johnson knocked on the closed door of room C- 3 and entered when a feminine voice called, "Come in."

Troy waited. Betty Jean and Dr. Johnson opened the door for him "Shenade is awake," Mrs. Johnson said. "You can go in."

Troy gulped, looked at the Johnsons, and then slowly crossed the room. He had to get right next to the bed before he could raise his head enough to see Shenade, now lying on a pillow. Troy caught a hint of a gleam in her eye when he glanced at her. A slow smile spread on her face. "Hi," she said.

Again Troy gulped. "Hi." Both looked at each other and then Troy blurted. "I'm so sorry, Shenade." He was almost crying.

A blank look covered her face when she spoke. "Mom told me what happened. I'm just glad you're okay."

"I thought you were dead." Troy cried as he slumped onto the chair next to the bed, his face now level with hers. She turned to look at him.

"I may not have a memory, but I'm a long ways from being dead. You can't get rid of me so easily."

"How can you be so flippant about it? You could have died."

"But so could've you. And we didn't. So—don't think about it."

Troy shook his head to hold back the emotion that filled his eyes with tears. As one escaped and rolled down his cheek, Shenade brushed it away with the touch of her hand. Troy grasped her hand in both of his. "I would have killed myself if you had died."

"Somehow I believe you." She pulled his hands to her lips and kissed them. "That's what makes you so special." Shenade looked into his face as if seeing it for the first time. "Actually, if you look in the mirror, you're the one that's the mess."

Troy quickly turned his head, forgetting that it hurt to move. "Hey!" Shenade squeezed his hand. "That was a joke. Don't take it so hard. We're alive and we'll be okay."

Shenade released Troy's hand when they heard movement from behind. "Your mother's going home now," Dr. Johnson said to his daughter as he and Mrs. Johnson re-entered the room. "Troy can monopolize your time."

"I'm staying till they kick me out," Troy told them.

"Don't get too tired," the doctor advised.

"I'll sleep in this chair if I have to. I'm not leaving.

"Shenade needs rest as well, Troy," Dr. Johnson said giving his daughter's covered toes a squeeze.

"She can sleep anytime. I won't keep her awake. I just want to be here." Troy slid painfully back into the large armchair.

"I'll go do my rounds, but I'll check in again before I go home."

"Thanks." Shenade said as her mother kissed her good-bye.

"How much do you remember?" Troy's attention went back to Shenade once her parents had left.

"Well, I'm not too sure. I don't know if the things I recall are things I do remember or things Mom told me. For awhile I couldn't remember from one conscious moment to the next, but I don't feel as lost as I did earlier."

Troy struggled to sit up. "Do you hurt?"

She turned to him and smiled. "Do you know what hurts the most?" He shook his head. "My ankle." Shenade stuck her bandaged foot out from under the cover.

Troy looked sorrowfully at it and then at Shenade. "Don't look so serious," she laughed. "It's not fatal."

"Yeh, but that injury is my fault."

"Why do you say that?"

"I overheard the paramedics in the ambulance mention your ankle injury. They said you probably got it when I pulled you out of the car."

"But Mom said you were concerned about fire. That you just wanted to get me out."

"But it was only steam and dust. Not smoke."

"But you didn't know that, Troy." She stopped. "You thought you were saving my life." Shenade leaned back and closed her eyes.

"Are you okay?" Troy reached out to touch her arm. "Should I call someone?"

"No, silly, but I think I'll take a nap."

Troy rested his head against the back of the chair.

"Troy?" Troy opened his half-closed eyes. "Thanks for caring so much. I'm glad you're here."

Troy tried to smile. ""I'm glad I'm here, too. Do you

want your head up?"

"No, thanks. It's too painful to put any pressure on my lower spine. When they got me up this morning and I put weight on my feet the pain in my back just about did me in." She was calm as she spoke.

"What is it?" Troy asked with concern.

"They're going to x-ray again on Monday once the swelling goes down." At Troy's serious expression she added, "I said not to worry. I'll be okay. Now let me get my beauty sleep or the nurses will boot you out."

Troy gave in, lying his head back again. Soon he drifted into a restless sleep. His dreams were interspersed with bits and pieces of the accident. Images of his father, Shenade, and mangled vehicles caused him to toss and turn fitfully, but fatigue and medication kept his body submerged in sleep.

A knock at the door sometime later aroused him and he heard Shenade call, "Come in."

Troy's body was stiff as he tried to straighten up, and pain ran from the soles of his feet to his ears. Resigning himself to the position he was in, he just opened his eyes to see the newcomers.

"Visitors!" Shenade exclaimed excitedly. "And bearing gifts at that."

"Hi, you two." Sam Livingston entered the room. "If I had known you'd be in the same room as your girl, Troy, I would have brought only one teddy bear. Oh well, have two. One for each of you so you can cuddle them instead of each other." He handed the blue bear to Troy and the pink one to Shenade.

"But you'll have to share the flowers," Kristin's voice carried from the door. "I'm not as rich as Sam. And besides," she teased, "I knew you'd be together. You two just belong together."

Shenade looked at Troy and they exchanged smiles. "Thank you," Shenade told them. "You shouldn't have done this."

"No, we shouldn't have." Sam rolled his eyes. "But you gave us quite a scare."

"Yeah," Kristin put in. "You ought to have heard the stories going around the gym during clean-up today. One story had Troy dead and Shenade paralyzed."

"And," Sam interrupted, "one had you both dead and Bob thrown from the car. It was unreal."

"So—" Kristin said more solemnly, "Sam and I decided to check it out for ourselves. We phoned your folks, Shenade, and your Mom told us."

"She said you had amnesia though." Sam leaned over Shenade's prone body and looked deep into her eyes. "But you don't look blank."

All four laughed. "She could never look blank." This was said by a new intruder.

"Hi, Carol," Sam straightened abruptly.

"I came to see if I'm wanted," Carol said almost fearfully.

"Why wouldn't you be?" Shenade asked, lifting her head to look at her. The flash of pain searing through her body made Shenade go pale, and she carefully lay back down again.

"Well it was me who got you to take Bob home."

"I volunteered," Troy interjected. "It was my decision."

"From what I was told," Kristin added, "no one could have prevented this accident except for the guy who ran you off the road."

"I wonder if they know who it was?" Sam's tone was more serious.

"I don't know," answered Troy.

"Didn't you see anything?" asked Sam again.

"It was too dark and I was trying to hold the car on the gravel. All I could see was orange courtesy lights on top of the cab."

Shenade reached out and touched Troy's shoulder. "So tell me what happened. I'd like to know so I can stop guessing. I don't even remember leaving the dance."

Troy looked at her hesitantly. "Are you sure?" he asked, more for his benefit than hers.

"Not if it's too hard for you," Shenade said sincerely.

Troy waited for a moment to collect himself and find the courage to speak. Then he started. "You and I had taken Bob home and were on our way back when—"

It took Troy some time to relate the incident as clearly as he could. When he finished speaking, all the room, which was now congested with visitors, became a mass of questions and comments.

"Excuse me!" a curt voice commanded from the doorway. "Visitors are limited to two and visiting hours are from one to five."

Like a parting of the Red Sea, the students, who now filled the room, divided, allowing the nurse to get to the bed. Some of the kids filed out but not before they called, "See you later."

"We'd better go too," Kristin said as she took Carol and Sam by the hands. "We don't want to get you two into trouble."

The nurse scowled as the drama class left the room. Troy, exhausted after reliving his ordeal, lay back in his chair.

"Are you planning on staying here?" asked the nurse cooly.

Troy looked at her fearfully and hesitated before answering. "Dr. Johnson gave his permission as long as I let Shenade sleep," he answered, trying not to sound rude or discourteous.

"Are you sleeping?" the nurse quickly asked Shenade, who now held Troy's hand in hers.

"I wouldn't sleep as well if Troy was gone," she answered kindly.

The nurse lifted an eyebrow at Troy and then her expression softened. "I'll bring you both some lunch, then I'd like you to rest."

"Thank you," both teens said at once. The nurse tidied the curtains before seeing the floral bouquet. Cupping the single rose in the middle of the flowers, she lowered her face and inhaled deeply. "Gorgeous," was all Troy and Shenade heard as she left the room.

Sunday came and went with an entourage of students from the school and church. Mr. Mac, Brother Matthews, Bishop Schmidt and his wife, as well as Troy's and Shenade's families came to visit. The only person he hadn't seen, Troy thought on his way home later that night, was Bob.

Chapter Thirteen

Shenade was not in her room when Troy arrived Monday morning. For an instant he panicked, then remembered the X rays. He was watching the ice crystals dance on the white lawn outside the window when he heard a familiar from behind. "Good morning, Troy."

"Hi," Troy greeted Mr. Mac. "Shouldn't you be in school?"

"I don't have a class until the second period, so I thought I'd come and talk to you and Shenade."

"She's not here." Troy pointed to the empty bed.

"I know. I just pushed her down to x-ray so I've talked to her already."

"Is something wrong?" Troy asked when he heard a hint of concern in the teacher's voice.

"Not wrong, but competitions are on Saturday and I wanted to see if you and Shenade are up to doing your parts."

"What did Shenade say? She still doesn't have her memory back."

"The only thing she can't remember now, it seems, is the accident. She says she'll direct from a wheelchair if need be." Looking straight at Troy, he asked, "What about you?"

"With this face," Troy responded sharply. "I should play

Frankenstein, not Liberace." Mr. Mac grinned and started to say something but Troy cut in. "And my back doesn't tolerate too much sitting on hard benches. And I still can't sit up straight."

"Well, you've mastered the music really well, and you work well with Shenade. I'd sure like you to try."

"How soon do you have to know?"

"Dress rehearsal's on Friday. If someone else has to play the piano they need time to practise. I'd like to know by school's end today."

"I'll think about it."

"We really need you, Troy," Mr. Mac emphasized as he left the room. "I'll stop by after school for your answer."

Troy's nod was his only reply.

"Hi," Shenade said. "I see Mr. Mac caught you, too." A nurse wheeled Shenade into the room and helped her to lie down.

"Do you really think you can handle directing this play?" Troy asked once Shenade was settled and the nurse had left.

"I think so. What did you tell Mr. Mac?"

"I said I'd think about it."

"Why think about it? You do a super job playing and we've worked out all the little kinks."

"Look at me," he grimaced. "How can I get in front of people with a face like this?"

"They'll understand, and anyway most of the time it'll be dark, or their attention will be on stage."

"I still don't think I can sit that long.

"I know," Shenade stroked Troy's arm when he sat down. "B—but I sure don't want to do it without you. I love working with you."

Troy placed his hand on Shenade's. She stopped stroking. They looked deeply at each other. Troy could not resist the desire to draw her hand to his lips. "I'll give it a try.

I guess we're in this together."

Dr. Johnson, who now stood in the doorway, cleared his throat. Troy immediately dropped Shenade's hand. Blushing, he slid back into the arm chair.

"Hi Dad," said Shenade, rising up on one elbow.

"Hi kids." Dr. Johnson came over to the bed. "I've just come from X ray." Troy gasped. Dr. Johnson did not miss the look of apprehension on the boy's face. "It seems," he said, "that when the car landed on its nose, the impact crushed a vertebrae here in your lower back." He touched Shenade's back through her pink pajamas.

"That's serious!" Troy exclaimed, his eyes never leaving Shenade's face.

Dr. Johnson continued, "I would say that if Shenade measured herself, she would find she is a half inch shorter, but once the inflammation is down, and the pain lessens, she should be fine."

"How can I be fine being a half inch shorter?" Shenade asked, a teasing gleam in her eye.

"I'm sure you'll compensate somehow," Dr. Johnson laughed, giving his daughter a one-armed hug. As he made his way to the door he added, "I've prescribed some medication for the inflammation and pain. It'll make you drowsy, but you need the rest.

Troy's eyes were still on Shenade when the doctor left. "I'm sorry, Shenade," he said.

"Don't say that again. I don't want to hear it."

"But—"

"But nothing. We're just going to get better together. Me, here in this bed, and you close to me in your chair."

Troy's mouth twisted into a little smile. "Okay," he said, and before he lay back, he kissed her on the forehead.

Troy changed into his gym suit before leaving for the play practice on Friday. His body was still stiff and sore and the gym suit was more comfortable than jeans. Bruising appeared blue, purple, black and yellow in places Troy didn't think had been hurt. His face, though, was the worst. Black and blue and green spread from his left eye down his cheek. Troy's cracked lips had healed enough for him to eat but the stitches in his mouth still pinched. What a mess, he thought as he combed his hair.

Troy picked the music from the dresser. Calling good-bye as he left the house, he walked to the Johnson's. Dr. Johnson put Shenade's wheelchair in the trunk of his car while Troy held the door open for her.

"You sure you can handle this?" he asked Troy.

"I'll go slow. And we'll come home right after practise."

"Call me if you need help," Dr. Johnson called as Troy got behind the steering wheel.

Troy pushed Shenade's wheelchair into the school, his music books in a sack hanging from one of the handles. As if on cue, as they entered the gym the drama class began to sing, "For they are jolly good fellows, for they are jolly good fellows, for they are jolly good fellows, which nobody can deny." Sam and Kristin came down the stage steps, each carrying a bouquet of flowers. Sam presented his to Shenade and Kristin gave hers to Troy. Both Shenade and Troy received a kiss from their flower bearer. "We're glad you're here," Sam said as they ran back to the stage.

Troy and Shenade were speechless and a little embarrassed. "Places please!" Mr. Mac bellowed, and Troy felt the tension lessen. Shenade began to wheel herself forward so he grabbed his book bag and made his way to the piano. "Good luck," he heard her call softly and they exchanged smiles before she continued on.

The piano had been uncovered and was turned so Troy could see the stage. He heard Shenade speak to Mr. Mac and then the teacher called, "Curtain's going up! Prelude, Troy!"

Troy's fingers hit the keys aggressively, setting the

mood for the upcoming scene. Sam Livingston was first to speak when the curtains opened. "Hi! My name is Flavius Maximus. I am a Roman private eye—"

Troy was able to follow his cues and have his fingers find the right keys until the end of Scene Two. His back refused to relax, and with the tension of trying to perform perfectly, Troy could feel the dull pain he'd learned to tolerate accelerate into spasms of agony. He tried to shift positions to release the tightness, but stabs of sharpness ran up his spine to settle in his head. His vision became blurred and he could hear the swell of sour notes as he misplayed the music. Once when no music was needed, Troy leaned his head on the piano. Just putting his head down took some of the tension from his lower back and legs, even though it was only temporary until he began playing again. Troy was getting frustrated. He was making a mess of things and twice they had to stop and redo a scene. The more Troy hurt, and the more mistakes he made, the more embarrassed and self-conscious he became. Frustration turned to anger and he struggled not to react. He wrestled with a desire to smash something. "I'm not going to let the anger win," he resolved. "Please, help me," he prayed softly and instantly he knew what to do. "I need a break," Troy said aloud to the actors on stage. The drama class watched him as he slowly and painstakingly left the gym.

"Take five!" Mr. Mac called.

Troy made his way to the bathroom. Taking some deep breaths, he leaned on the cupboard. He was so engrossed in his thoughts he did not hear the door open.

"Troy?" the voice was soft but husky.

Troy lifted his head and his eyes met the questioning expression on Bob Green's face. "Are you okay?" Bob asked. Before Troy could answer... "I don't blame you for being angry at me," Bob said as he leaned on the wall and fidgetted with the towel dispenser.

"I'm not angry with you. At least not now." Troy took in a deep breath, more to help ease the pain in his back than to make a point. "I was. When I thought Shenade was going to die I wanted to punch your lights out for putting us in such a predicament." He took another breath, feeling his muscles relax a little. "Then I realized it wasn't you who ran us off the road...Is that why you didn't come to visit us in the hospital?"

"I was so afraid," Bob said, his head hung low. "The neighbors told my folks the morning after the accident that you were dead and that Shenade was paralyzed." He stopped as Troy looked directly at him. "I just wanted to die."

Troy placed a hand on Bob's shoulder. "I really was angry with you. Every time my stitches pinched, or I tried to move, I wished you had been in the car too. You know, so you could have suffered."

Bob cringed. "You've no idea how many times I wanted to be with you. I told Carol I would never drink again—that is, once she would speak to me."

Troy chuckled, "Well, if that's the one good thing learned from all this, then I guess it was worth it. Come on," he slapped Bob on the back, "we'd better get back."

Bob held the door open for Troy and the two boys walked back toward the gym. "You know I felt guilty every time I looked at you. And when you started to make mistakes on the piano, I realized they began when I came on stage."

Troy stopped at the gym door and turned to Bob. "You never even crossed my mind. My back started to hurt and my fingers wouldn't work. I knew I had to take a break or I'd lose it."

"And you're really not angry with me?"

"No. Anyway, how could I be angry with a friend?"

"You're my friend too," Bob said emphatically. Placing a hand on Troy's shoulder, he added, "We all like you."

A heavy silence filled the room as they entered the gym. As soon as the class saw Bob and Troy talking together, a steady chatter began. Shenade was sitting in her wheelchair directing students to their places. "You know something, Berringer? Somehow you've snagged the neatest girl in the high school. I could never imagine why, but now I know. You are two of a kind." Bob left Troy standing speechless by the piano and bounded up to the stage.

Troy sat down and began to play. His fingers moved more easily, his pain more tolerable. The rest of the evening went by quickly.

Not long after the practice was over, Troy found himself alone with Shenade, Mr. Mac, and Bob. "I'm closing the school," the teacher told them all. "You kids need to go home and get some sleep. Tomorrow's a big day."

Bob helped Troy cover the piano and the three youths left the building. "Take good care of him, Shenade," Bob called as he slid into his car.

Once Troy had Shenade settled in the passenger seat of her father's car and the wheelchair in the trunk, Shenade spoke, "What was Bob's comment about? Do you need to be taken care of?"

Troy chuckled, "I think he's a little jealous. I believe he likes you."

"But he wants me to take care of you?"

"Oh, who knows," Troy laughed as he manoeuvered the car through the lot.

Shenade kept her eyes on the road as Troy left the parking lot and pulled onto the street. The traffic was heavy and the activity on main street was busier than normal. Shenade had gone very quiet, so when Troy stopped at a traffic light he turned to glance at her. She sat with her hands covering her eyes. "Are you okay?" he asked.

"I suddenly have a nasty headache. Right here." She lifted her head and pointed to the center of her forehead.

Troy leaned over. "Right there?" He faked a kiss.

Shenade smiled but carried on. "I think it's the traffic

lights or the motion or something."

"Close your eyes. I'll have you home in a jiffy."

The traffic stayed heavy and Troy felt the strain on his body. Thinking he would take a side road away from the congestion, he flipped on his left signal light as he approached the next intersection.

"What's the matter?" Shenade asked, when they had stopped at the red light.

"I'll cut over a block and get out of the bright lights and traffic."

"That's a good idea."

The light turned green and Troy eased into the intersection. Out of the corner of his eye he caught sight of a set of headlights advancing quickly from the right. Its speed made Troy feel uneasy and he sensed danger. He couldn't turn until the oncoming traffic cleared. The approaching vehicle was racing toward them, red and blue flashing lights close behind.

"He's not going to stop!" yelled Shenade and with a cry she buried her head in her hands.

Troy slammed his foot onto the accelerator and the car shot forward. The siren screamed past behind them and Troy quickly moved the car to the right and parked on a side street. It wasn't until the noise was gone that Troy became aware of the soft crying next to him. With his adrenalin pumping, his heart still in his mouth, Troy painfully pulled himself over beside Shenade and put his arm around her. She turned, burying her face in his flannel jacket. Her crying turned into uncontrollable sobbing. He held her tight. "I'm sorry," he cried.

After a few minutes, she lifted her head. "Oh, Troy! I was so scared."

"You're safe now," he said. "I won't let anything hurt you." He held her tighter.

"No, Troy," she whispered, a sorrowful look in her eyes.

"I remember."

"Remember?"

"I remember the accident. The lights, the gravel, the grass flying toward us!" Shenade stopped. "And the blood!"

"Oh, Shenade." He buried his face in her sweet-smelling hair. "I'm so sorry." Both teens cried openly and unashamedly now.

Finally Shenade spoke. "You don't have to be sorry, Troy.I know it wasn't your fault. I feel so foolish for crying like this."

Troy wiped his face with his sleeve. "It's okay. E—even I feel better."

"Maybe we needed the cry," Shenade said, looking up into Troy's eyes.

"Maybe." Troy kissed her nose quickly, holding her for a moment. "I was so afraid that car would hit you and I couldn't bear it if you got hurt again.

"But you did well stepping on the gas like you did."

"Guardian angels were watching over us," Troy said running his fingers through her long, silky curls. He felt warm all over, his heart so large he thought it would explode. "We should probably go home now," he added reluctantly.

"Probably," Shenade replied without conviction.

Troy released her with a smile and pulled the car away from the curb. They talked about Bob and the play all the way to the Johnson house.

Once they were parked in the driveway, Shenade said, "You're sure different since the accident." She caressed the back of his hand.

"In what way?" Troy's heart beat a little faster.

"Almost..." she kept her eyes on their hands, "like you...oh, this sounds silly."

"Go ahead."

"Well you seem more grown-up...more settled or some-thing."

He lifted her chin. "I don't know how grown up I am, but I do feel like I understand a few more things. The accident has shown me how things can change so fast—how fragile life is and how precious and short.

"I understand that," Shenade put in meekly. "I guess we all feel invincible until we see death coming at us.

"We sure have to live life with a lot of faith, don't we."

"It seems so because too many unforseen things can happen."

Troy and Shenade sat thoughtfully for a few minutes. Shenade spoke first. "I want to thank you for being so tender and kind when we had the accident. I remember waking up and seeing lots of blood but the only thing I felt were your hands stroking my face." Shenade looked tenderly into Troy's eyes. "I love you, Troy" she said.

"I love you, too. You've given me lots to live for."

"You're going to make a real good missionary and stake president some day, you know, and I want to be around when that happens."

Troy smiled at Shenade but drew back. "I—I think I'd better get you inside now." His heart was pounding.

"I haven't upset you, have I?" Shenade didn't sound anxious.

"No, I just think this has been a big night for both of us."

"I suppose so. We do have competitions tomorrow." Shenade's smile was warm and she leaned over to kiss Troy's cheek. "Come on, help me inside."

Troy helped Shenade into the house, giving her one more kiss before leaving her.

The light was on in Joanie's bedroom when Troy got home.

"Is that you, Troy?" his mother called.

"It's me, Mom!" He went to her room. An unused syringe and alcohol swab lay on a white tissue on the bed cover. "Are you okay?" he asked.

"Yes. I'm just getting ready for bed. How did it go tonight?"

"It was wonderful." He went to the bedroom window and looked out in the direction of the Johnson home.

"Are you going to be okay to go to the competition tomorrow then?" Joanie came to stand beside him.

"I wouldn't miss it even if I had to crawl," Troy said as he gave her a quick hug. "And you know what, Mom? I love it here. This is where I belong."

Troy left without seeing his Mother's tears of gratitude.

Judy Ann Crawford

Biography

Judy, a freelance writer, is a regular columnist in the Taber Times and has published articles and short stories in a variety of publications including, ProLife Magazine, Alberta Scoutlook, Arizona Senior World (Gilbert, Arizona, USA), Lethbridge Living Magazine, and others.

She is a creative writing instructor for Taber Adult Learning Council and Brooks District Further Education Councils, and for numerous writing groups, and does readings in the local schools.

A Business Management graduate of Brooks Campus, Medicine Hat College, Judy has also taken a Writing Fiction course from Independent Study BYU, and is a graduate of Quality of Course Writing School in Ottawa, Ontario, Canada.

Currently Judy is a member of the Oldman River Writers of Lethbridge, Alberta, the Writers Guild of Alberta, the Canadian Authors Association, and the Lethbridge Children's Literature Roundtable.

A mother of five sons and one daughter, Judy currently resides in Taber, Alberta, Canada where she has taken up writing as a full-time career.